The Guns at Three Forks

TERRELL L. BOWERS

A Black Horse Western

ROBERT HALE · LONDON

© Terrell L. Bowers 2004
First published in Great Britain 2004

ISBN 0 7090 7518 9

Robert Hale Limited
Clerkenwell House
Clerkenwell Green
London EC1R 0HT

Typeset by
Derek Doyle & Associates, Liverpool.
Printed and bound in Great Britain by
Antony Rowe Limited, Wiltshire

CHAPTER ONE

'I don't think this is a very good idea,' Dave Kenyon told his much younger brother, Cory. 'You're going to get all three of us tarred and feathered.'

Cory laughed. Like most boys at sixteen, he was brazen and reckless.

'Loosen your cinch, Davy.' he dismissed the concern. 'We're going to live here for a long time. Me and Adam want to check out the girls.'

Adam, a year younger than Cory, shook his head.

'I don't know, Cory. It sure ain't worth getting a whupping just to look at a bunch of girls. They're liable to beat us to within an inch of our lives and toss our battered bodies into a cactus patch!'

'Hey, you two sissies don't have to come along,' Cory replied. 'I didn't ask for any company.'

Dave uttered a derisive grunt. 'Funny, that's not the way it sounded when Mom said for me to keep an eye on you.'

'OK, OK, but this is a town affair and I want to have a look around. It isn't like I'm going to ask some girl to dance,' he grinned at Dave, 'not unless one of them gives me the eye.'

'A black eye is what you'll get.' Dave remained cynical.

'Davy's right,' Adam concurred. 'We're about as popular around town as a sack full of smallpox. This is asking for trouble.'

But Cory had his mind made up and Dave was obliged to watch out for his brother. He knew the idea was dangerous, but they had to eventually start mingling with their neighbors. Their father, a Yankee officer, had been assigned to a post nearby and decided to settle in Three Forks, Texas. As such, the family would have to find a way to fit into the ex-Confederate population.

When they reached town, the livery barn was ablaze with light, as lamps burned brightly both outside and inside the largest structure in town. There were a dozen wagons parked about and a number of horses were tied at the hitch rail. From inside the barn there came the sound of music and chatter.

Previously the three Kenyon boys had accompanied their mother to several Sunday meetings. Their reception had been cool, but Mrs Kenyon was an amiable sort and had worked hard to make friends with the locals. For herself, personally, she had managed to melt away some of the resistance over their being from a Northern state. As for the three boys in the family, they had yet to get a civil word from anyone.

Dave tied off his horse at the stable fence. His brothers did the same, then the three walked toward the front entrance.

'I knew it.' Dave spoke to his brothers. 'See the shiny rig by the side of the barn?' At Cory's nod, he said: 'It belongs to Rex Jardeen.'

'Rex ain't so tough.' Cory discarded his concern. 'I'm betting you could take him in any kind of fight.'

'Ma's idea in having me come along with you was to prevent any of us from getting into a fight ... remember?'

Cory dismissed his concern and led the way inside. Once through the door, he paused to look around. Dave and Adam moved up to his side and the three of them observed the festivities.

Two men were making music from a corner of the barn, an old gent with a fiddle and a one-legged man with a string guitar. A woman was also seated at a piano, a few feet away from the pair, playing accompaniment. Dave recognized her as the one who played music at the Sunday meetings. The melody was lively and there were several people out in the middle of the barn floor, dancing. Some were kids or teens, but there were two young couples and three gray-haired pairs in the mix.

Cory smiled broadly. He had recently become interested in girls and was busy checking out the number of younger females in the crowd. Dave swept his eyes over the room too, being watchful for any sign of trouble. However, when he spied one particular girl, standing next to the punch bowl, he could not look away. He recognized the pert little blonde at once. She was decked out in a slightly faded pink gown with ruffled sleeves and white lace about the collar and matching trim on the flounce near the hem of the dress. The outfit had obviously seen its best days, but it did not distract from the girl's bubbly exuberance. Having taken a special notice of her a time or two before, he paused to admire her from afar.

Jenny Moran was her name and she struck him as a spunky young lady, as cute and feisty as a kitten playing with a piece of string. She had a smile on her face, as she conversed with a tall, rather broad-shouldered, man. Dave was only able to see him from the back, but he recognized Rex Jardeen, the town bully. He and Rex had exchanged a few heated words previously. There was nothing cordial about their relationship.

'Did I mention this was a really bad idea?' Adam whispered, taking notice of the number of hostile stares being directed their way.

'They can kill us, but they can't eat us,' Cory quipped. 'That would be downright uncivilized.'

'What about chopping us into pieces and feeding us to the vultures?' Adam asked.

'It was a dry ride into town,' Cory said. 'Let's get us a drink at the punch bowl.'

'We'll more likely get punched ourselves!' Adam complained.

Dave took a deep breath to calm his dread and took the lead. They passed along the outer rim of the dance floor and a number of the dancers or bystanders paused to glare at them. Rex must have noticed the sour looks. He rotated about and scowled when he spotted them. His expression was instantly one of arrogance and malice, while Jenny

8

appeared more surprised that Dave and his brothers would dare to attend a town function.

Dave pulled up short of the refreshment table, as several boys had moved to block their path. Rex, still holding Jenny's hand, stormed over to take charge of the group.

'You ain't welcome here, Yanks,' he announced testily.

'Howdy,' Dave replied with a smile, ignoring the outward hostility. 'Looks like a good turn-out for the dance tonight.'

'I done said no one invited any Yanks.' Rex's tone was belligerent.

'You could use a little work on your tough-guy line,' Dave replied easily. '*I done said* doesn't sound very literate.'

'I'll maybe show you some *literate*!' Rex threatened.

Dave looked past him and touched the brim of his hat in a polite gesture to Jenny.

'Good evening, Miss Moran.' He purposely displayed his best smile. 'May I say, you look like the belle of the ball tonight.'

A hint of crimson crept into Jenny's cheeks, but she was not allowed a response. Rex pushed her aside and placed himself in front of Dave. His chest puffed up and he bore into Dave with glowing, hateful eyes.

'I done said you ain't invited here, Yank,' he stated emphatically. 'You best git, afore me and my friends here give you a helping hand.'

Dave took a short appraisal of Rex. They were near the same age, but Rex was a couple inches taller and about thirty pounds heavier. Rex had a barrel-sized chest and thick shoulders and arms. He was a pushy, loud-mouth sort, who thought a great deal of himself. Being the most sizable man in all of Three Forks, he was used to pushing most everyone around. The others in the group were closer to Cory's age, mostly in their mid to late teens. They all looked primed for a fight.

'We only stopped by to listen to the music and have a glass of punch.' Dave attempted to defuse the confrontation. 'We didn't come here to start any trouble.'

'What about the smell?' Rex sneered. 'I can smell the stench!'

Dave grinned. 'I noticed it right off too, but I didn't want to say anything about your hygiene in front of the lady.'

Rex blinked at the reply. 'I don't know what *hygiene* is, but. . . .'

'I suspect that's obvious to everyone here tonight,' Dave quipped, before he could finish the sentence.

Rex balled his meaty fists and took a step forward. 'Look here, you dirty—'

But Jenny grabbed hold of his arm. 'Stop it, Rex!' she reprimanded him. 'If the blue-bellies want to listen to the music and have a drink of punch – let them. We don't want a fight to spoil the dance.'

'Take my word for it,' Rex snarled, 'it wouldn't be much of a fight. One punch would do it!'

Dave bobbed his head in agreement. 'He's right there, miss. I reckon one good punch and your loud-mouth friend would be out like a busted lamp.'

'You think so?' Rex roared. 'How about we all go outside and see how tough you are, Yank?'

'There's only six of you against us three,' Dave taunted. 'You think those are good enough odds for you to have a chance of winning?'

'Stop it!' Jenny snapped, pushing forward until she was between Rex and Dave. 'Both of you! We don't want any fighting here tonight!'

Dave used an apologetic tone of voice. 'Like I said, we didn't come looking for trouble. We're neighbors now, whether anyone in Three Forks likes it or not. We Kenyons would like to put our past differences aside and be sociable.'

'You're a bunch of blue-belly Yankees,' she replied icily. 'Don't expect us to roll out the welcome wagon for you.'

Dave sighed. 'The war ended over a year ago, miss. We have to learn to live together as one people again.'

'Tell that to your father and the low-life, Yankee troops who harass and molest us Texicans at every turn.'

'My father is not part of those unsavory and undisciplined soldiers,' Dave argued. 'We only want to get along.'

Jenny's own anger and defiance rose to the surface. She glowered at Dave, lifting her chin, proud and haughty.

'We don't need you to be spreading your cow-leavings here, Yank! You came to the dance with a single purpose in mind – to start a fight!'

Dave met the fire in her eyes with a disarming

11

equanimity. He even coerced a slight smile to curl at the corners of his mouth. When he spoke, his words were polite and inviting.

'I may as well 'fess up and tell the honest truth, Miss Moran. Cory wanted to attend the dance so he could look at the girls, Adam wanted to listen to the music, and I was kind of hoping for the chance to take a spin around the dance floor with the most beautiful young lady here tonight.' His smiled widened. 'I suspect that would be you.'

Jenny was totally unprepared for his flattery. She stood agape, words failing her. Even as she sought some sort of response, Rex yanked her back to stand at his side.

'The gal is with me,' he sneered. 'She's with her own kind.'

Dave doffed his hat and displayed a complete sincerity.

'If that's the truth of it, Miss Moran, you have my deepest condolences. I fear it's going to be a long and boring evening for you.'

'Let's get them, Rex!' One of the boys pushed forward, ready to fight.

'Yeah!' Another growled his accord. 'We'll knock the stuffings out of all three of the Kenyon boys!'

Rex knotted his fists. 'You asked for it, Yank!' he declared. 'We're gonna tear—'

'Rex!' Tom Delton's forceful voice stopped everyone in their tracks. Tom and his wife ran the local store. He had obviously been watching the potential showdown and now stepped over to separate the group of locals from the three brothers. He pushed through until he was able to place himself between Rex and Dave. Then he took up a determined stance, folded his arms and regarded them with a stern look on his face.

'Let's not spoil the evening ... *gentlemen.*' He spoke a warning Rex and the others from town. Then, pivoting about, he cast a hard look at Dave. 'And you, Kenyon, you knew you wouldn't be welcome here. Why did you come?'

'We were only trying to be sociable,' Dave told him. 'After all, we live here too.'

Tom studied him for a moment, evaluating the truth in his eyes. After a few lengthy seconds, he returned his attention to Rex and the gang of local boys.

'Break it up, you fellows,' he warned. 'There'll be no fighting here tonight.'

'Come on,' Jenny tugged at Rex's arm. 'Let the Yanks have their drink and be on their way.'

The other boys grumbled a few threats and oaths as they backed away. Tom waited until they had moved off, then rotated about to again confront Dave.

'No fighting, no trouble ... understand?'

'It's like I said, Tom. We only want to be neighborly.'

Tom uttered a sigh. 'All right, but don't stay too long,' he warned. 'I've gotten to know and respect your folks, but most of the people in Three Forks aren't ready to be neighborly just yet. If you make trouble, it'll only take longer to win them over.'

Dave gave a nod of his head and Tom went back to

his waiting wife. Another tune filled the air, so they began to dance.

Rex and Jenny had also migrated out to the dance area and started to move about together. Dave took some satisfaction in the fact that Rex had about as much rhythm as a pig skating on a patch of ice. He bobbed up and down, out of time with the music, while Jenny was forced to make a real effort to prevent her feet from being trampled.

'That was close,' Adam said, letting out the breath he'd been holding. 'I figured sure we was going to get our branches pruned.'

'Let's have a glass of punch,' Dave suggested.

'I ain't all that thirsty,' Adam said. 'You two don't have to stick around for no lemonade on my account.'

But Dave led the way over to the punch bowl and picked up a glass. Cory and Adam followed his example and they each had some of the refreshment.

Dave continued to watch those dancing. He sorely wished he could be out on the floor, especially if he could have danced with Jenny Moran. There was something special about her. Besides which, he wanted to break the ice between the townspeople and his family, to make friends and be accepted. Being a family of outsiders and ostracized by everyone in Three Forks was a real pain . . . and downright lonely.

They were through with their drinks by the time the dance number ended. Rex made a point of swaggering in their direction again. He led Jenny by the arm and stopped at arm's length from Dave.

'Time's up, Yanks,' he said arrogantly. 'Get going, before we strap you to the back of a rail and ride you out of town.'

'You wouldn't be so tough if you didn't have a dozen guys to back your play,' Cory sneered at him.

'Get out of here, runt!' He snarled at Cory, 'I even catch you looking at one of our girls and I'll bust your head like a ripe melon!'

Rex reached out to give Cory a push, but Dave caught hold of his wrist.

'You lay a hand on one of my brothers and you'll answer to me.'

Rex jerked his hand back. 'Get going, Kenyon.' He haughtily raised his voice. 'Leave while you still can.'

Dave hooked a thumb toward the door and glanced at Cory.

'Let's go.'

'Hold on, Davy!' Cory cried. 'You're letting this clown act like he's as big as his mouth. I ain't gonna run from him like some yella dog!'

'We didn't come here to start trouble, Cory. And we aren't going to ruin the dance for everyone, simply because this bellowing oaf hasn't got the manners of a warthog.'

Rex took a threatening step. 'I'll show you who has manners, Yank!'

Jenny put a restraining hand on the bully's arm.

'Stop it, Rex!' She used a scolding tone. 'They're leaving! Let it alone.'

'Talkin' ain't gonna get me no satisfaction,' Rex boasted. 'I'm going to whip me a Yank.'

'Do you want me to agree to your proposition or

not?' she said pointedly.

Rex simmered down at once.

'You mean it?'

'Only if you let the Kenyon boys alone.' At his obedient nod, she turned her attention toward Dave. 'You said you didn't come to start trouble.'

'It isn't us doing the pushing.'

'You're pushing your luck by being here at all,' she told him. 'You've had your look around and a drink from the punch bowl. I think you had better leave.'

'We ain't going to be told what to do!' Cory exclaimed. 'We got a right to be here. We live in Three Forks too!'

Dave put a governing hand on his younger brother's arm.

'The young lady is right,' he said. 'We've had our look. It's time we were leaving.'

'Tuck your tail and scoot!' Rex sneered his words. 'You ain't welcome here.'

Dave knew to reply would start the conflict all over again. He didn't want that. Even if Rex was man enough to fight him one on one, it was a no-win situation. If he lost to him, the jeers would only be worse the next time they came to town. If he won the fight, it would add to the hostility from the others.

He led his two brothers out of the barn, unable to shut out the sound of several boys shouting catcalls after them.

Cory spun on him once they were out into the dark of night. He was livid.

'I never took you to be no coward, Davy!'

'We have to try and get along with them, Cory. We

16

won't make peace if we end up in a fight every time we come to town.'

'Did you see the way they looked at us?' Adam could not hide his fear. 'I thought we was dog-meat for a minute.'

'Yeah.' Cory was still mad. 'Lucky we were able to *tuck our tails and scoot,* just the way Rex told us to!'

'Mom is making progress with some of the folks.' Dave attempted to explain the logic. 'If we sent a couple boys home with black eyes, their folks would be dead-set against our family all over again. You don't win people over by fighting with them.'

'Well,' Cory said, 'I, for one, ain't going to take being run off lying down.'

'What's that mean?' Dave wanted to know.

Cory stormed over and grabbed up the reins of his horse.

'You'll see,' he said harshly. Then he sprang aboard and put his horse into a run, disappearing into the darkness.

'Where's he going?' Adam asked Dave.

'I don't know. I hope he doesn't get himself in to a pile of trouble.'

'We going to follow him?'

'We'll take it slow and easy on the ride home. Let's hope he'll catch up with us.'

CHAPTER TWO

Jenny hated the idea of allowing Rex to see her home. Not only would her mother be mad about her having the bully escort her home, but it was going to be a major chore to avoid being kissed. Rex was one of the few bachelors in the Three Forks area old enough to court her . . . unless she considered Dave Kenyon. Both of them were three or four years her senior.

If not for the gravity of the moment, she might have laughed at the comparison. Her mother would only be upset at her allowing Rex to drive her home. If she had allowed the Yank to see her home she would have had apoplexy!

Kip Moran, her younger brother, walked over to her when Rex wandered off to talk to one of his friends. With him out of hearing distance, Kip put a serious look on his face.

'I'll follow behind you and keep Rex's wagon in sight,' he whispered.

'You needn't be that obvious. Rex knows better than to try anything,' Jenny assured him. 'If he does get frisky with me, I'll get off his wagon and wait for you.'

'OK, but Mom is going to be mad. We were supposed to come to the dance together and return home the same way.'

'If she doesn't hear us come in, she won't have to know.'

'I don't get it,' Kip said. 'You ain't all that fond of Rex. Why let him take you home?'

'It was the only way I could prevent him from fighting with the Yank.'

Kip waved a careless hand.

'I'd as soon let him give it a go,' he told her. 'Rex has always been the biggest bully around town. It wouldn't hurt for him to get taken down a few notches. Maybe Dave Kenyon would have taught him a lesson or two.'

Jenny raised her eyebrows at her brother.

'You sound as if you would have been cheering for Kenyon!'

Kip shrugged his shoulders.

'Like I said, Rex has pushed all of us younger guys around since we were kids. As far as Kenyon goes, he's never uttered an off-color remark or given me a second look. I would have enjoyed a chance to see Rex get his due.'

'I didn't want to see anyone fighting.'

'Yeah, so you took up the fight for the Yank and now you're stuck on the ride home with Rex. Seems to me you're the one taking the beating.'

Rex returned at that moment. The band had finished playing for the night, so the dance was breaking up and everyone was starting to leave. Rex had a triumphant look on his face.

'Come on, Jenny,' he gloated. 'Time for me to see you home.'

She flashed her brother a look of regret, then stepped over next to Rex.

'We better not dally. My mother is going to be up and pacing the floor.'

Rex took her by the hand and headed for the door, leading her along like a pet on a leash. She wondered at his lack of tact. Didn't he know a lady and a gentleman were supposed to walk arm-in-arm?

Rex did think to give her a hand up into the wagon – after he first untied the horse from a hitch post and almost climbed into the buckboard himself. Jenny scaled her way aboard and moved over to sit at the far end of the buckboard seat. It wasn't until Rex sat down that they both became aware of something sticky and slimy on the bench seat.

Jenny stood up, at the very moment that Rex let out a grunt of surprise.

'What the hell. . . ?' he caught himself before swearing. 'What's this?' he bellowed, rising up on to his feet. 'It looks like—'

'It's axle grease!' Jenny lamented, brushing at the goo which covered the back of her dress. 'Someone smeared grease all over the seat! My dress is ruined!'

'It was them worthless Yanks!' Rex wailed. 'I'll kill them dirty skunks!'

'Mother is going to be furious!' Jenny cried. 'This is my only good dress.'

Rex was more concerned with his own trousers.

'I swear, I'll get them Kenyon boys!' he ranted. 'They are going to pay for this!'

Kip heard the commotion and pulled his wagon up alongside Rex. 'What's the matter, Sis? What is it?'

Jenny climbed down from the wagon and picked up a handful of powdery dust from the street. She started to rub some of the dirt on the soiled material.

'My dress,' she sniffed, about to cry. 'The whole back is covered with grease.'

Kip saw she couldn't see to do a good job, so he jumped down from his wagon to help.

'Help me coat some dirt on the grease,' she told him. 'It might keep it from penetrating the fabric.'

'Those blue-coat scum!' Kip growled. 'I can't believe they'd do this to you!'

Jenny was also fuming over the prank. She shouldn't have gotten mixed up in the feud between Rex and the Kenyon boys. Her payment for playing the role of mediator was to have her dress ruined.

'It's a mess,' Kip said, after rubbing some of the dirt into the material. 'I don't think even lye soap is going to wash it out.'

'Mom's going to kill me.'

'It ain't your fault, Sis.'

'I wasn't supposed to ride with Rex. This happened because I was on his wagon!'

'Yeah,' Kip admitted. 'I doubt even those low-down, no-good Yanks would have done this to you on purpose.'

'Let's get on home.'

'What about Rex?'

'He's going to be busy cleaning the grease from

21

his wagon for a while. He can't expect me to wait around for him all night.'

Kip nodded his head.

'Wait a minute, while I run into the barn. I'll get a gunny sack for you to sit on. We don't need to get any grease on our own wagon seat.'

Jenny swore under her breath.

'I'm so mad I could spit nails! This is the only decent dress I have to my name and now it's completely ruined!'

Dave heard the approach of a horse and looked back over his shoulder. Cory appeared, riding hard, from out of the darkness. Catching up with them, he reined up his horse and fell in alongside Dave and Adam.

'Well?' Dave asked. 'What mischief have you been up to the last half-hour?'

'Me?' Cory pretended innocence.

Dave stared at him through the gloom of the night. 'Don't play that game with me. I know you better.'

'It was a great idea,' Cory began. 'I would have made you proud.' Then he lowered his head shamefully. 'That is, it was a great idea, until . . .'

Dave waited, but Cory did not continue.

'Until what?'

His brother uttered a dejected sigh.

'It isn't my fault. I didn't know your girlfriend was going to ride home with Rex.'

'What are you talking about?'

Cory told them about having smeared axle grease on Rex's wagon seat. Then he related how Jenny had sat down and gotten it on her dress.

'Of all the stupid stunts!' Dave lamented. 'We've been working for weeks to make friends with these people and you go and pull a stunt like this!'

'I was only aiming to get back at Rex.'

'Yeah, and start a new war for us to fight.'

'He asked for it!' Cory argued. 'The guy's always playing the big man and pushing us around. He talks to us as if we are lower than dirt!'

Dave was sickened at the thought of doing anything to hurt Jenny Moran. He had hoped that, with time, she might accept his family as friends.

'This is great,' he muttered. 'Jenny sticks up for us and you end up ruining her dress!'

'I'm telling you, Davy, I didn't have no idea she was going to ride home with Rex. I was only after him.'

'It's too late to change it now.' Adam eventually spoke up. 'Maybe Mom can stop by and explain to Mrs Moran that Cory didn't mean for the prank to include her daughter.'

Dave was already thinking of how to make this thing right. He had been saving his money for a new saddle. If he acted quickly, maybe he could defuse the situation before it got out of hand.

Jenny shook out the wet pair of trousers and pinned a leg to the clothesline. As she attached the second leg, she felt an odd prickling at the back of her neck. She spun about, suddenly aware she was not alone.

Dave Kenyon was standing a few feet away. He had a package in one hand and quickly removed his hat with the other.

'There's no need to shout for help or make a dash for your gun,' he told her hastily.

Jenny cast a quick lance at the house, but her mother was busy with cooking and could not see the clothesline from the kitchen.

'You've got a world of nerve, showing up on our place!' Jenny told him, hedging her words with ice. 'If ever a man deserved to be horse-whipped. . . .'

'I didn't come here to cause any trouble.'

'You mean like the dance Saturday night? That's what you said then too, wasn't it?' She glowered at him and instilled an icy vehemence into her words. 'Then you greased Rex's wagon seat and I ended up with it all over my best dress!'

Dave gave a negative shake of his head.

'I didn't know anything about the prank until after it was over,' he said. 'Cory was upset about being run off. He wanted to get back at Rex.'

'You'd better git!' she warned him. 'If my mother or brother were to see you. . . .'

'I'm leaving,' he said, but he bent at the waist and placed the package on the ground. 'I only came by to drop off a peace-offering,' he explained, straightening back up. 'Mrs Delton says you can exchange this for another color or she'll make any adjustments you need.'

Jenny frowned, wondering what the shop-owner had to do with the mysterious package.

'Mrs Delton?'

Dave remained serious, twisting his hat nervously in his hands.

'Again.' His voice was quietly apologetic. 'I'm real

24

sorry for what happened.'

Jenny continued to glare in silence as Dave backed up a step, replaced his hat and then disappeared around the side of the house. A moment later, she heard a horse going down the lane at what sounded like a lope.

She set down her laundry basket, walked over and picked up the package. Carefully, she began to unwrap it. Even as she tore the paper away, she sucked in her breath in wondering surprise.

The item was light blue, smooth as satin to the touch, with a delicate ruffle of white lace. She shook it out and discovered it to be a brand-new dress. It wasn't just as pretty as her old one – it was ten times nicer!

Jenny could not suppress her excitement. She hadn't had a new dress since the last Easter before her father and elder brother went off to war. Six years ago!

She held the garment up to measure it against her body. She was in that very position when her mother appeared from out of the back door. The woman stopped in her tracks and stared in shock.

'I heard a horse leave the yard,' she said. 'I didn't know what to think.'

'David, the eldest Kenyon boy, brought it for me,' Jenny told her, turning around so she could get a look at the garment. 'It's payment for his brother ruining my only good dress.' She held it in place. 'What do you think?'

Her mother did not smile.

'You can't be serious, Jennifer! I won't let you take

a present from one of them dirty Yanks!'

'No!' Jenny was defensive at once. 'It isn't a present, Mother. It's compensation for an unwitting mistake. Cory Kenyon was trying to get even with Rex. He didn't know I would be on his wagon.'

The news caused another frown to contort her mother's face.

'You were supposed to come home with Kip.'

'I told you the way it was. I was trying to prevent a fight.' She paused to smile at the way the sun's rays enhanced the color of the dress. 'Besides,' she got back to the business at hand, 'it was Cory who pulled the prank. David Kenyon said he didn't know anything about it . . . and I believe him.'

Her mother's ire was quelled at watching how happy she was with the new piece of clothing.

'It's curious, but I looked at that very dress the last time I was in town,' she admitted. 'I remember wishing I had money enough to buy it for you.'

'Humm, guess that shows the older Kenyon boy has good taste.'

'It *is* a ravishing gown,' Mrs Moran admitted.

Jenny saw her mother's resolve fading at seeing her so delighted about the gift. To take advantage of her momentary weakness, she whirled about, holding the dress tightly, with one hand on the waist and the other up to her throat.

'Isn't it beautiful?' she instilled the excitement she felt into her voice. 'I can't wait to try it on.'

'This is an awkward situation,' her mother said. 'How can I let you accept such an extravagant present from one of those Yanks?'

Jenny lifted her chin.

'There's no reason why I shouldn't take it,' she argued. 'It was their fault my dress was ruined.'

'What about the rest of the town? You know what everyone is going to say.'

Jenny knew this was going to be difficult, but she was determined to keep the beautiful gown.

'We don't have to tell anyone how I got the dress,' she said.

It was obvious her mother did not wish for her to give up the dress. Her fear was that word would spread and everyone would think they were joining the ranks of the Yankee family.

'You're sure this older Kenyon boy didn't know about the grease?'

'Yes, I'm sure, Mother. He isn't the sort to pull a prank to get back at Rex. If he had wanted to get even with Rex, he would have done it with his fists.'

Her mother snorted. 'He'd have gotten his head busted. I'd guess Rex is probably thirty or forty pounds heavier than the Yank.'

'I don't know, Mother. David stood up to Rex and didn't seem the slightest bit afraid of him. Kip seemed to think he might be up to the job, too. Yank or not, he isn't afraid of Rex.'

The woman pushed a strand of hair out of her face. She had aged a great deal since the deaths of her husband and eldest son. Jenny could see she was weighing the options. If her mother insisted, she would have to return the dress.

'Please, Mom.' She hurried to sway her thinking. 'This isn't a present, it's an offer of apology, a simple

27

payment for ruining my dress. It's only fair that I keep it.'

Her mother succumbed at last. 'All right, Jen. You can keep the dress, but you can't tell anyone how you got it.'

'What if Mrs Delton tells someone?'

'I need to go to the store and see if they ever got in any more salt or sugar. While I'm there I'll ask her to keep this matter private. If anyone should ask, you need only tell them the dress is a replacement for the one that was ruined by the grease. They don't need to know it was purchased by a Yank.'

'Yes, yes!' Jenny agreed instantly. 'I can do that.'

Her mother smiled, a gentle compassion softening her features.

'Maybe you ought to try it on, in case it needs some alteration?'

Jenny tucked the clothing under her arm and sprang over to hug her mother. Then she sped into the house. They didn't own a large mirror, but the one in her mother's bedroom would allow her to see her reflection. She knew the dress was going to wear beautifully. For the briefest moment she wished David Kenyon would have stuck around. Wearing such a gorgeous dress, she knew she would be . . . what had he called her at the dance?

Oh, yes, the belle of the ball!

CHAPTER THREE

The summer heat came early in the day down near the Texas border. Dave had been out before daylight, hunting along the mesa for fresh meat. It was an hour before high noon and he had only two rabbits to show for his morning's work. He had seen a few wild cattle, but the deer were few and scattered along the low mountain range. It was a good thing his family didn't have to rely on what he brought home for food.

He stopped his horse in the shade of a rocky overhang to let the animal rest. Sitting there, he considered how much better off he and his family were than most of the others around Three Forks. It was hard to blame the people for resenting his clan. His father earned actual money, so they were able to buy necessary food and supplies. The same could not be said for many of the locals. The people were mostly broke from the long years of civil war. The battle between the Union and Confederacy had depleted their resources and killed or crippled a great many of their men. All across the state there were abandoned farms and ranches; many of the plantations remained run down or deserted. The ranch they now owned was one which had fallen into ruin, after the two brothers running it had gone off to fight in the war. Neither of them had returned, so Dave's father had been able to purchase it for what was owed in back taxes.

Dave could not keep his thoughts from returning to the dance and how the main suitor for Jenny Moran was the town bully. He doubted a blow-hard like Rex would be a young lady's first choice for a dance partner. If Dave hadn't been considered to be the enemy, she might have agreed to dance with him.

He smiled to himself, wondering what her reaction had been to the dress he'd bought for her. He had explained to Mrs Delton how ruining Jenny's dress had been an accident and she promised not to tell anyone about the purchase. As relationships went, the Deltons were among the few who didn't openly resent the Kenyon family. Of course, it helped that his family was able to pay cash for their supplies. With so little money in Three Forks it was a big help to their little store.

'It's going to take some time,' he said aloud. 'Once they get to know us, we'll make friends and be accepted. Just got to be patient.'

Dave's horse perked his ears forward, but it wasn't from his muttering. Dave paused to gaze off in the direction his horse was looking. He ducked down when he spied three riders on the trail below. Smoothing a hand along his mount's sleek neck, to keep him from sounding a whinny in greeting, he whispered:

'Easy, boy, we don't want to introduce ourselves to those fellows.'

Staying well back in the trees, Dave remained out of sight, then began to shadow the trio. He suspected from their dress that they might be up to mischief. All wore sombreros, which shaded dirty, unshaven faces. They had ammo-belts, strung in criss-cross fashion over their chests and each wore a gun on one hip and carried a machete-style sword on the other. They had the appearance of bandits, perhaps sizing up the next town or ranch they would ravage and loot. He hoped that they were simply three unsavory-looking riders, passing through, and not looking for trouble.

Regardless of their motives, Dave kept watch on them from the ridge, using the natural cover of the rolling hills and gullies, careful to not show himself. While he had seen little actual fighting during the war, his father had taught him military tactics and he was a superb shot with his Henry rifle. He was capable in a fight.

The trail made a sharp turn and Dave was close enough to get a good look at the three men. He studied the trio more closely and felt a icy pit form in his stomach. They were hard, desperate-looking men. He worried that they might belong to a larger group of bandits or even the cutthroats known as *comancheros*.

The *comancheros* were reputed to be a mixed bag of half-breeds, Indians, Mexicans and white outlaws. It was thought that anyone with a price on their head could join the pack of raiders. They evaded the law by staying in Mexico most of the time, but occasionally they crossed the border to raid loot and kill.

The Union had sent upwards of 100,000 soldiers to occupy Texas. However, the troops were stationed there to control the rebellious Texas population, not to police marauding Indians or chase after a handful of bandits. It was a tough time to be a Texas citizen.

Dave knew from experience that it was equally tough being a blue-belly Yank. He and his brothers would have had more friends if they had stayed at the fort. However, his father wanted to start a place of his own, a place he could call home. He chose to buy the small ranch at Three Forks, so that his family could become a part of Texas.

'Yeah, right,' Dave muttered, thinking of the near-fight at the barn dance and the constant name-calling he and his two brothers had encountered around town. They were about as welcome as a spooked skunk at a church social.

Dave continued to follow the men for the better part of a mile and was at last able to discharge a sigh of relief. The trio had made a turn at the junction in the road, heading toward the Mexico border. He was thankful they didn't head in the direction of his ranch or the town of Three Forks.

The relief was short-lived. He saw the dust of a wagon, coming down the trail from the nearby foothills. Someone had probably been up gathering timber for firewood. The route they were traveling was going to cause them to intersect with the course chosen by the three scroungy-looking men.

Dave's heart began to pound. An immediate tightness clutched his chest. Fearful there was going to be trouble, he reached down to the scabbard and pulled out his Henry rifle. Then he began to circle below the crest of the hill, working to get closer to where the rough-looking men would meet up with the wagon.

'Watch the ruts, Kip!' Jenny complained, after a jarring bounce. 'You drive worse than if you were blind and drunk!'

Kip laughed his teasing mirth.

'Oh, yeah? When was the last time you rode with a blind drunk?'

'The last time I let you have the reins!' she retorted.

'Well, I'd let you drive the wagon, but we need to get home before the end of the week. I've watched snails tread past us on occasion when you were on the reins.'

'You put us into the ditch, from being reckless,' she warned, 'and I'm not going to help you unload the wagon to get it back on to the road.'

Her younger brother laughed again.

'Old Nester ain't going to put us into the ditch.' he referred to the horse in harness. 'She might be as old as dirt, but she knows to keep to the middle of the trail.'

'Nester is about as blind as an earthworm, too. What makes you so sure she can even see the middle of the trail?'

Kip started to reply, but suddenly jerked back on the reins and used the brake, forcing the loaded wagon to skid to a lurching, uneven stop.

Jenny didn't ask what he was doing, for she also saw three men on the trail. They were sitting with their horses standing crossways to block the way. She sucked in her breath, instantly frightened.

Two of the men looked them over for a moment, while the third one eased his horse to Jenny's side of the wagon. His piggish black eyes roamed over her body like so many dirty fingers.

'Say there, *señorita*,' he said, leaning from the saddle to leer at her more closely. 'What's a purty little thing like you doing out here all alone?'

Kip displayed an inordinate bravery.

'She ain't alone,' he announced testily. 'She's with me.'

A second man moved his horse to Kip's side. He was a large man, dark of skin, either from his heritage or from long hours in sun and several layers of dirt.

'That's right, Pudge.' He mocked Kip, while also leering at Jenny. 'The gal ain't alone. She's done got herself a real tough escort.'

'What do you say, little woman?' the one called Pudge ignored Kip. 'How about having some fun with us?'

'She's only fifteen.' Kip was the one to reply, lying about her age. 'She's my younger sister. You touch her and the whole country will be down on you for molesting a child.'

Pudge grunted his disbelief.

'If she's fifteen, I'm your grandma, Fryer.'

Fryer chuckled, displaying a smirk.

'You don't think the kid would tell us an outright lie, just so's he could protect his big sister from us vulgar sorts?'

'The boy probably hasn't learned to count yet,' the third man put in. 'He isn't but knee-high to a grasshopper himself.'

Fryer bobbed his head up and down and spoke to the man who continued to block the way with his horse.

'That's sure enough the truth, Juan. What do you think? Should we have some fun?'

Juan passed the back of his hand along his mouth, wiping it with anticipation.

'We can let them pass. . . .' he began. Then, with his wicked eyes glowing: 'Providing the young lady here pays the toll.'

Fryer chortled in his throat.

'What do you say, gal?' he asked Jenny. 'One kiss each and you and the squirt can continue on your merry way.'

'I'd sooner kiss a trio of snakes!' Jenny exclaimed, trying to muster strength into her voice. 'Leave us be!'

Kip attempted to slap the reins and start Nester moving, but Fryer was too close. He stuck out his foot and pressed it against the handbrake. With the wheel locked, Nester surged forward against the traces, but could not start the wagon rolling.

'I was up Louisiana way, some years before the war.' Pudge spoke up. 'I remember how them Southern ladies all had polite manners and a sweet way of talking to a man.' He grinned at Jenny.

35

'Mayhaps you Texican gals ain't had no proper upbringing.'

Jenny was growing more apprehensive with each passing second.

'Please, gentlemen.' She tried to reason with the men. 'Let us pass. We have to get home.'

'Sure thing, honey,' Pudge said. 'You can continue on your way . . . soon as you give us each a sweet little kiss for the toll.'

Kip grabbed the horsewhip and stood up.

'You let us alone!' He drew back the whip, threatening to use it on Pudge. 'Or I'm going to part your hair with this!'

But Kip was looking at the wrong man. Jenny cried a warning, but too late! Fryer drew his gun and clouted Kip over the back of the head with the pistol barrel. Her brother sank down on to the wagon seat from the blow. Jenny began to tend to Kip, fearful of how badly he was hurt. However, she felt the wagon sag on one side and discovered that Pudge had dismounted his horse. He was climbing into the wagon after her!

Jenny screamed and scrambled over the seat and into the bed. She maneuvered about three steps across the pile of cut timber, before Pudge tackled her. The two of them tumbled out of the wagon and landed on the dirt road.

Jenny kicked her way loose and leapt to her feet. She attempted to run, but the men were too quick to react with their horses. Fryer bolted his mount forward and raced up alongside of her. Before she could escape into the brush, he reached out and caught hold of the back of her work dress. With a vicious yank, he pulled her upward and off her feet. Then, as she began to flounder about, he let go and sent her sprawling on to the ground. Jenny used her elbows and forearms to keep from landing face first on the dusty trail.

Jenny quickly regained her wits and hurried to crawl away from Fryer. However, Juan jumped down from his horse and blocked that direction. Before she could get up, he grabbed a handful of her hair in one meaty hand and jerked her on to her feet. Jenny twisted about and began to swing at him with tightly balled fists.

'Holy cats!' Fryer shouted gleefully. 'Watch her, Juan! You've got a wild she-devil on your hands!'

'Get her, Juan!' Pudge also guffawed. 'Don't let her get the best of you!'

Jenny was strong from hard work, but she was only two inches over five feet in height and a hundred pounds soaking wet. She was completely over-matched against a full-grown man.

Pudge arrived from behind her and caught hold of her flailing arms. He pinned them around at her back and prevented her from using her fists or nails. Fryer moved in from the other side, a sneer on his lips.

'Fighting only makes it all the more fun for us,' he said.

'Pucker up, sweetheart,' Juan jeered, moving directly toward her from the front, licking his lips, preparing for a kiss.

Revulsion impelled Jenny into action. She lashed

out with her foot and kicked him solidly in the knee!

Juan howled from the pain and limped around in a circle. Pudge laughed loudly at his misery, until Jenny also stomped down on his foot.

'Hot-dang!' he wailed from the sharp pain. 'That ain't funny!'

Pudge released his hold on her, but Fryer was there to prevent her breaking free.

'Enough of this foolishness!' He snarled the words.

There was a flash before Jenny's eyes and she was stung by a brutal swat along the side of her head. It carried enough force to knock her down on to her hands and knees.

Dazed and stung by the vicious jolt, bright lights detonated inside her head, while she blinked at tears which blurred her vision. Before she could gather her senses, she was surrounded by the three men. She felt herself dragged to her feet and was unable to fight back.

God, help me! she prayed silently. *They are going to hurt me!*

CHAPTER FOUR

There came the sudden crack of a gunshot and Fryer's hat flew off of his head. All three men stopped, frozen in a moment in time, each searching for the shooter.

'The next bullet will be a couple inches lower,' a commanding voice boomed. 'Let go of the girl and step away from her!'

Fryer picked up his hat and moved a few feet away. Pudge hesitated, but then stepped over to join him. Juan, however, abruptly drew a skinning knife and threw an arm around Jenny. He pinned her in his grasp, searching the brush for the ambusher.

'Come out where I can see you, bushwhacker!' he shouted. 'Or else I'm going to butcher this little strumpet right in front of your eyes!' Juan twisted Jenny about, using her as a shield. She squirmed and struggled, until he pulled back her hair and raised his knife, placing the blade over her right ear. 'What do you think, bushwhacker?' Juan called out. 'Think the girl's hair will cover the fact she hasn't any ears?'

Jenny froze, a scream of terror on her lips, but

fearful of making a sound. In her mind's eye she remembered a soldier she had once seen, one who had been hit by a piece of shrapnel. He had worn his hat low, but it could not hide his missing ear. Would she be forced to wear her hair long, combed out to hide her own disfigurement?

'I'll take off this one first,' Juan snickered, 'so you know I'm serious!' His voice grew thick and menacing. 'Let's see how long you can stand to watch me skin this little Jezebel, bushwhacker!' He took a quick look, ready to start slicing with the knife. 'Here goes the first ear. . . .'

Jenny bit down on her lower lip to stifle her cry from the searing pain. But the sound of a rifle firing cracked the still air once more.

Time seemed to stand still. Juan's knife was poised in his fist, ready to begin his savagery; the other two gunmen were standing nearby, hands on their pistol butts, ready to draw and shoot. Jenny was prepared for the terrible agony of having her ear removed. Then, after the echo of the rifle's report, everything grew silent.

It seemed an eternity, but it lasted only a split second. The bullet had struck Juan in the head. His grip on Jenny went lax and he dropped to the ground like a sack of potatoes.

The other two men had their hands on their guns, both were staring in the direction of the gunshot. But neither made a move to draw his weapon.

Jenny's heart instantly restarted and she moved hastily away from the fallen body. Shaking with fright, she uncertainly reached up to see if her ear was still intact. To her relief, it was still attached to the side of her head.

'You've got one chance to live,' the voice sounded again. 'Drop your guns, load your stupid dead friend on his horse and get out of here. Try and draw your pistols and you can join your pal in hell!'

'You see him, Fryer?' Pudge whispered out of the side of his mouth.

'Somewhere off to our right,' Fryer replied, 'but I didn't see the muzzle-flash.'

Pudge took note of the man on the ground.

'He nailed Juan right between the eyes, Fryer. The man's a crack shot with that gun.'

'Make up your mind,' the voice came again. 'Toss your pistols or try your luck.'

Fryer slowly lifted his hands, palms outward in a sign of surrender.

'All right, fella!' he said. 'You got us! We're leaving.'

'Guns first . . . and no tricks,' the voice warned. 'I've got a bead on you both.'

Fryer and Pudge each removed their handgun and dropped it on the ground. Then Fryer caught up the horses. Without knowing the who or where of the man in the nearby bushes, their only option was to follow his orders. Once Juan was strapped over his horse, they climbed aboard their own mounts.

'You so much as look back over your shoulders and I'll knock you out of the saddle!' the voice cautioned them. 'Don't stop until you're back across the border.'

Fryer paused a last time to scan the expanse of

41

sage and buck brush.

'You have no idea who you've killed, my friend,' he said, baring his teeth in a sneer. 'Juan Gervaso was an important man.'

'Threatening to cut off a woman's ears makes him stupid, not important,' the voice replied. 'Ride out, before I change my mind about letting you live.'

The two men led the third horse behind them and started down the trail. After a short way, they kicked their horses into a run. The dust rose from the galloping animals, as they rode hard to get out of rifle range.

Jenny watched the disappearing riders, still quivering from the attack. She was short of breath and felt on the verge of breaking down and sobbing. However, she fought for self-control and hurried around the wagon to see if Kip was all right.

Kip was conscious, sitting up under his own power and rubbing the knot on the back of his head. Tears of pain glistened in his eyes, while he quickly surveyed Jenny from head to foot.

'You all right, Sis?' he asked, clearly concerned about her welfare. 'They didn't hurt you, did they?'

'Nothing serious,' she said, gingerly touching the side of her face, where the one man had struck her. 'Help arrived before they got too carried away.'

Kip looked past her and groaned. 'Gall-durn the luck!' he said sourly. 'Bring back them vile, dirty bandits! Anything would beat us having to be beholding to Yankee scum. It's Dave Kenyon!'

Jenny whirled about and saw him now. He was on foot, leading his horse with one hand and carrying a rifle in the other. He continued to maintain a watch beyond their wagon, keeping an eye on the distant riders.

'Did I hear him right?' Dave asked. 'Did he say the dead man was Juan Gervaso?'

'Yes, I think that's the name,' Jenny replied. 'Where did you come from?'

Dave explained, as he walked up to join them.

'I've been following them for the last mile or so.'

'Were you wanting to join their gang?' Kip taunted. 'Those border trash sorts ain't much worse than you miserable blue-bellies.'

'Kip!' Jenny snapped at her brother. Then, instilling a calm reason in her voice: 'Why don't you go over to the ridge and make sure those men keep going.'

Her brother glared at Dave, but he was used to doing as his older sister ordered.

'Sure, Sis,' he muttered. 'I'll watch 'em.'

Kip tied off the reins so Nester wouldn't start to move, and jumped down from the wagon. He immediately put his hand up to his head again.

'Whoa!' he moaned, 'don't let me do anything that sudden again for a spell.'

Jenny was instantly worried about him. 'Are you all right?'

'Only if you've become twins,' he joked, blinking at the ache in his head from the jarring movement. 'I think there's going to be two of everything for a bit.'

'Can you see OK to watch those men?'

Kip waved his hand to dismiss her concern.

43

'I'm OK, Sis.' Then he hurried off through the tangle of brush, working his way out to the crest of the hill, where he could see the valley floor and watch the riders.

Jenny waited until he was out of hearing distance before she risked eye-contact with Dave Kenyon. He was taller than she remembered from their previous meetings, probably close to six foot. Lean, yet stalwart, he was not altogether hard to look at. Rawboned, there was power in his muscular shoulders and arms. She also noticed he seemed to exude a distinguished authority. He had the kind of face which was moderately handsome either clean-shaven or with a mustache. The eyes looking back at her were a cloudy gray, steady and reserved.

'I guess I owe you my life,' she began. 'Or, at least, an ear or two.'

'Did he cut you?'

She pulled back her hair to show him. 'Nary a nick in the skin . . . thanks to you.'

'I didn't know how else to stop him.' Dave was apologetic. 'I would have had no chance against the three of them if I had come out in the open. Besides which, they would still have had you as their prisoner.'

'Yes, I-I approve of your actions, Mr. Kenyon,' Jenny told him. 'I don't know what kind of mischief those two men had in mind, but I'm sure it was going to be unpleasant.' She hesitated, as if it was difficult to find the words, then added: 'Thank you for your help.'

'Those fellows are my enemy.' His voice was

passive. 'Same as yours.'

'Yes, but you didn't have to get involved.'

A dark frown was cast over Dave's expression.

'You might think of us Yankees as selfish, low-life critters, gal, but we don't stand by and watch while a young woman is mistreated or abused.'

'But you will grease the seat for a lady to ruin her dress!' she threw back at him.

'That wasn't me,' he insisted. 'I told you, Cory was the one responsible for smearing grease on Rex's wagon seat.'

She swallowed her anger. 'I'm sorry. I shouldn't have said that.' Then, with a subtle lift of her hands: 'It's just after all the years of war and hate. I can't help feeling the way I do.'

'The war is over.' Dave stated the obvious. 'I know it isn't right for the Union to send soldiers into Texas to ride herd on the people here, but not all of us are arrogant bullies or maggot carpetbaggers. My father was assigned to a post here; he wanted a home, a place for my mother and us boys to live. That's the reason why he bought the ranch.'

'My father and brother were both killed at Vicksburg,' she told him. 'If we dislike Yankees, it's because your side took away the men we loved.'

'Good men died on both sides,' Dave replied gravely. 'In a war between brothers and neighbors, there can't be any winners, only losers. Fighting and killing one another should never be the way to settle differences.'

'You certainly killed Juan quick enough.'

'I was afraid he wasn't bluffing,' Dave explained. 'I

didn't dare wait until he started cutting.'

Jenny didn't know what to say to that. However, when Dave turned around to get on his horse, she knew she had to stop him.

'You asked about the dead man, Juan Gervaso,' she said. 'Did you recognize his name?'

Dave paused before answering: 'I'm afraid he's probably related to Angel Gervaso.'

Jenny recognized *his* name.

'You mean the notorious bandit leader?'

Dave pivoted around to look at her again.

'The last time my father was home, he spoke of him. He told us there is a band of killers and thieves who call themselves *comancheros*. They raid wagon trains, rob stages and have attacked settlements on both sides of the border. They steal, plunder and kidnap people for ransom. They'll sell guns to the Indians or to either the Mexicans or French, who are currently fighting a war for control of Mexico. Our troops can't cross into Mexico to chase them after they make a raid in Texas, and the Mexican army can't cross into Texas when they raid in Mexico. They play the border like kids play the safe zone in Run-Sheep-Run.'

Jenny was vaguely familiar with this variation on the game of tag.

'I've heard of the *comancheros* too. It seems that none of your Yankee pals are overly concerned about catching or punishing them.'

'I suppose it might seem that way.'

She was struck by a new dread.

'You don't think they were looking over Three

Forks? They wouldn't attack our town?'

'They burned Gloryville to the ground a month or so ago,' Dave replied. 'Looted the whole town and set fire to it. My father says those people were left with nothing but the clothes on their backs.'

'Can your father offer us protection?'

Dave grunted. 'I haven't seen him in three weeks. His troops are so busy putting down Texicans who riot or fight against the military's authority that they don't have time to chase after the Indians or *comancheros.*'

'The war was supposed to settle the issue about all people being free,' Jenny stated harshly. 'Does that mean only the Negroes or Yankee supporters? Don't the people who backed the Confederacy have any right to reclaim their own lives?'

'Texas never agreed to the surrender,' Dave answered. 'In some circles, the Union's presence here is considered a military occupation.'

'And, of course, it's easier to guard against a few helpless Texicans, than fight against marauding Indians or bandits like Gervaso – is that what you're telling me?'

Dave sighed, outwardly weary of the debate.

'I don't wish to argue politics with you, Jenny.'

She furrowed her brows, immediately offended.

'I never gave you permission to call me by my first name.'

Dave went to the side of his horse and returned his rifle to the scabbard. Then he took a moment to pick up the extra pistols from the ground and also stuck them into his saddle-bags. He mounted his horse,

47

ready to ride, before he looked over at her to answer. There was a slight upward curl at the corner of his mouth, as he studied her.

'I reckon, when I rescue a maiden in distress,' he said carefully, 'it earns me the right to take some liberties.' Then with an added grin, 'Even if she hates me for being from the North.'

Jenny felt the warmth of the sun on her shoulders, but it was the heat rising up into her cheeks which nearly overwhelmed her.

'I did thank you for your help.' She maintained a degree of decorum. 'Perhaps, one day, I might be able to look at a Yankee and see him as something other than the vile scum of the earth.'

Dave chuckled. 'Is that your idea of a compliment?'

'I was trying to be polite.'

He continued to grin. 'If that's being polite, I'm sure glad you weren't being sarcastic.'

Jenny shook her fist at him. 'You're a pig-headed Yank!' she flared up at him. 'I won't be made fun of! Not by some no account, sneaky—'

Dave cut her name-calling short. 'Be seeing you . . . Jenny.'

'My mother would skin you alive for calling me by my first name without permission!' she shouted.

'Do I have your permission?'

'No!'

'All right then,' he said, 'I'll call you something more befitting.' With another of his impish grins, 'How about Sparks?'

'What?' She was aghast.

'It fits,' he answered back. 'Every time you look at me, I can see the fire in your eyes. And whenever we speak or get close to one another, the sparks start flying. Yep, Sparks it is.'

'David Kenyon!' she snapped. 'You are a most irritating and exasperating person!'

'Whatever you say, Sparks.'

'And stop calling me by such a childish name!'

'So long . . . Sparks.'

Jenny glared at Dave Kenyon, but he whirled his horse about and put it into motion. The two remaining bandits had made a show of leaving, but he neck-reined his horse in the direction they had taken. She knew he was going to trail after them for a few miles. He wasn't going to take a chance on having them double back and cause more trouble.

Even as he vanished over the hill, her brother came wandering back toward the wagon.

'I watched as long as I could see them,' Kip reported. After a moment, he regarded her with a suspicious smirk. 'Guess your white knight will keep an eye on them long enough for us to get home.'

'We'd better get started.' She dismissed Kenyon from her thoughts. 'How's the head?'

'It feels like a fair-sized melon, one that was dropped off the wagon during harvest. I guess I'm not much of a hero.'

'You stood up for me,' Jenny praised him. 'That was a brave thing to do.'

'Brave or stupid?' he asked. When Jenny did not make a reply, he added: 'Regardless, it's a good thing the Yank was around to lend a hand.'

'I suppose the Kenyon boys aren't as bad as most of the Yankees around Texas.'

'You mean because he's old enough to come courting and a handsome sort to boot?'

Jenny frowned at Kip. 'You go giving me a hard time, little brother,' she warned, 'and I'll swat you hard enough to make that smack with a gun feel like a love-tap!'

'Gall-durn!' Kip exclaimed, not the slightest bit afraid of her threat. 'You've done got a soft spot for the Yank.' He began to laugh. 'Wait'll Ma hears about this.'

'If you go telling Ma I've a soft spot for Dave Kenyon, I'll make you sorry you were ever born!'

'My, my,' he teased, 'you sure do set up a holler sometimes. Does that Yank know you've got such a temper?'

She didn't answer Kip, but climbed up on to the wagon. Even as she sat down, she had to smile to herself. Dave must think she had something of a short fuse. Why else would he have given her the nickname of Sparks?

Jenny took up the reins and waited for Kip to get seated. Then she released the brake and flicked the reins to get Nester started.

'Ah-h-h, you're not going to drive?' Kip complained.

'You told me you were seeing double. I don't want you taking a turn in the road that isn't there.'

'But you go so dang slow, it'll be dark before we get home and unload this timber.'

'Serves you right for picking on me.'

Kip grumbled under his breath. Jenny couldn't make out the words, but she was able to let out a sigh of relief. Her terror and panic was already a fading memory, but the way Dave Kenyon looked at her . . . that was going to remain with her for a long time.

Angel Gervaso had started small; he, his cousin Juan, and three others. They mostly ran guns and sold them to the Comanche. As they came into more money and became more bold in their conquests, the number of his followers grew. Renegade Indians, mixed-breed outcasts, a couple runaway slaves, several escaped criminals and even a few deserters from both the Confederacy and the Mexican army had joined his band. They were known as *comancheros*, but Gervaso liked to think of his gang as a small army of revolutionists. They were an independent force, fearsome and bold, striking terror into the hearts of their victims.

The problem was, with the swell of his followers, Gervaso was forced to seek greener fields and richer targets. It was a difficult task to feed, clothe and provide guns and ammunition for thirty or forty men. They could no longer rob a single store or trading post, but now had to pillage an entire town or village. It was a worrisome task, to provide for such a large group.

Fryer and Pudge had returned during the night. They had brought in the body of his cousin. Juan was buried quickly, deep enough so the coyotes would not dig up his bones. He and Juan had never been very close, usually doing more fighting and arguing than anything else, but he was still going to miss him.

The next morning he picked up his breakfast on a tin plate, walked over and sat down beside Fryer and Pudge and waited for their report.

'We never saw the man who shot Juan,' Fryer told him. 'He hid in the bushes and shot without warning.'

'And you two ran away?'

'We couldn't see him and you saw the body. He nailed Juan square between the eyes. A crack shot like that, with us unable to see him, what could we do?'

Angel and Juan had started the gang together. They often split the gang and went on different raiding parties. He would have to find someone else with whom to entrust the chore of secondary leader. Rather than discuss the episode further, he got down to business.

'What about the town of Three Forks?'

'It looks as easy as Gloryville,' Fryer said. 'We counted very few men on the streets or working in the shops. It is mostly old people and some women and children.'

'That's right,' Pudge agreed. 'It looks as if they were hit hard by the war. I'd guess most of their fighting men were crippled or killed.'

'None of the army boys around?'

'With so few fighting men in town, the blue-coats don't have to worry about them,' Fryer replied.

'What does Three Forks have to offer for us?' Gervaso asked, stuffing a strip of salt pork into his mouth and beginning to chew.

'The store was small, but the owner said they were expecting a delivery of goods. There is a tavern too. They had a fair supply of liquor and several barrels of beer.'

'Enough to make it worth our while?' Gervaso wanted to know. 'Gloryville was not much of a prize. I don't wish to attack a second Texas town and get the Union army down our necks for such a small amount of loot.'

'Even if they call for help from the army,' Pudge discarded his concern, 'it takes but a few hours for us to slip back across the border and be out of their reach.'

'We don't want a war with a lot of killing,' Gervaso told them. 'A man doesn't butcher the sheep which provide him with wool.'

'I doubt these people would be so stupid as to fight,' Fryer surmised. 'They are in the same fix as those in Gloryville. They know it would be a fatal mistake to oppose us.'

'I agree,' Pudge contributed. 'The town is ripe for harvest and we didn't spot but a couple who might put up a fight.'

'What about nearby? Any large ranches or plantations?' Gervaso wanted to know.

'Hardly a place with any grown men around,' Fryer replied. 'Most of the places are being worked by women and kids.'

Pudge bobbed his head in agreement.

'Yeah, we saw nothing but old men and a few cripples; that's about it.'

Gervaso looked at the hole in Fryer's hat, then at

the vacant holsters on the two men's hips. 'You gave up your guns after Juan was killed?'

'We had no choice,' Fryer admitted.

Pudge joined in with their defense. 'He put the first slug through Fryer's hat and the second between Juan's eyes. That was one guy who could shoot.'

'So he kept your guns?'

Fryer explained about stopping the wagon to get more information about the town. In the process, the assailant had sneaked up and gotten the drop on them. Juan had tried to draw and been killed for his efforts.

'We could have taken the bushwhacker, but we never did see where he was hiding. The only way to locate him would have been to draw against him too. Then he would have killed one of us, while the other tried to spot his position.'

'My cousin and a couple of my top men,' Gervaso said bitterly, 'bested by some gun-slick you don't even get a look at.'

'He stayed hidden from view and proved he could shoot.'

'What if he has friends who can also shoot?' Gervaso asked.

Pudge uttered a grunt of contempt.

'He's only one man. Once we know who he is, we take him out of the fight.'

'I agree,' Fryer said. 'If we get rid of the sharp-shooter, the rest of those around town will fold like a pair of duces.'

Gervaso paused between bites. 'I've got scouts looking at two other places, both Mexican villages.

Juan was supposed to take care of Three Forks on his own. If the town is such easy pickings, maybe you boys could take a few men and ransack the place on your own.'

'Sure, we could do it.' Pudge was agreeable. 'I'm sure word has spread about what happened at Gloryville. There ain't no one going to dare and put up a fight against Angel Gervaso's band.'

'Take Keen and Chico . . . Red too. Will it take more than the five of you?'

'Ought to be plenty to take what we want from a town like Three Forks,' Pudge said, giving a confident wave of his hand. 'We'll take a wagon and a couple pack-animals for the loot.'

'You boys rest up a couple days. We're having a little celebration over by the mission tonight, so you enjoy yourselves and leave when you get everything ready. If you run into trouble, the other scouting parties will be back pretty soon. If we should need to attack in force, we'll be at full strength in a week or so.'

'We shouldn't have any trouble at all, Gervaso,' Pudge bragged.

'Yeah,' Fryer joined in, 'we'll be back with everything of value, before our scouts even return.'

Gervaso gave them a grunt of satisfaction, but remained skeptical.

'First off, you'd better pick up some guns. Even sheep balk at giving up their wool to a man without a pair of shears.'

The two men left and Gervaso finished up his meal. Fryer was smart and Pudge had good horse sense in any kind of fight. He didn't doubt they were capable, but he wouldn't rely on them completely. Looking around, he caught the eye of the man called Sauvage. He was also known as the French Butcher, labeled a criminal by both the Mexican government and Emperor Maximilian because of his unbridled savagery. Gervaso had saved him from a firing squad. He owed his life to Gervaso and had no friends or loyalty to anyone else in the world.

Sauvage came over and waited for orders. Gervaso used his mastery of several languages to speak to him in French. He ordered him to prepare for a ride. His job would be to follow Fryer and Pudge at a discreet distance. He would be there to see their raid went as planned.

The man said nothing, asked no questions. He gave a nod of understanding and moved away. Gervaso did not have to mention also the second reason for keeping an eye on his men. There might come a time when part of his band was off on a job and came into a fortune in gold or found something else of great value. His followers were bandits and thieves, so it would not be out of the question for them to take their plunder and not return. Sauvage was his insurance against such a thing ever happening.

Gervaso wondered how the war in Mexico was going. He had heard rumors that Maximilian was struggling to maintain his financial support from the French government. If his troops were not paid, the war would turn quickly. Once Mexico was under a single rule, he and his men would be targets of the new regime.

Considering such a possibility, he needed to score a few big pots before the end of the revolution. Once the French began to withdraw, he would use his small army to help finish them off. He could then declare himself a general and offer his services to Juárez. Enough wealth would secure him a place of power within the new government.

He knew he had to grab all he could, while there were no American or Mexican armies to interfere. Three Forks might not be rich, but the spoils would pacify his men and fill their bellies with food and beer. For the time being, that would have to do.

CHAPTER FOUR

Mrs Kenyon read the letter aloud to the boys, as she always shared word from their father. William was involved in overseeing a military tribunal in El Paso, where there had been some trouble. He would be tied up for at least another week.

When she put down the page, Dave could see the slight smile on her face. He knew his father had written a personal message at the end of the letter. He always did.

'Your father's service date is up in a few more months,' their mother began. 'If he feels we have a good chance to make a go of our place, he will resign his commission to work the ranch. He's grown tired of being in the army ... especially since being assigned here in Texas.'

'It was a long war,' Dave commented. 'I was sure glad to be mustered out when it ended.'

'A man has to look for the future of his family,' she explained. 'He has served his twenty years in now, so he will receive a pension. With this ranch, we should be able to make a decent life for all of us.'

'Yeah, buying the ranch was a real popular move with the people in Three Forks too,' Cory complained. 'Me, Davy and Adam have a marvelous reputation around town. There go the Kenyon boys,' his voice was thick with sarcasm, 'nice family, except for being dirty, rotten, blue-belly Yanks.'

'The healing will take time,' Mrs Kenyon admitted. 'We can help by attending the church meetings and trying to break down resistance against us. As for myself, I was invited to join the Ladies Social Circle last week. It's a step in the right direction.'

'They asked you because you were the only one around town with any money,' Cory said. 'No one else could afford to help buy the school supplies they need.'

She remained patient. 'David will want to take himself a wife one of these days. It's sure to help us settle into the community.'

'Unless they hang him for fraternizing first!' Cory said.

'David is a man,' she answered. 'You boys should try and follow his example.'

'It ain't fair!' Cory exclaimed. 'You shouldn't have waited eight years to decide to have me and Adam. We'd all three be men by now.'

'Yes, and probably one or two of you would have died in the war.'

'Davy came through without a scratch.' Cory dismissed her concern. 'I bet me and Adam would have done the same.'

'The fact remains,' their mother continued, 'we must learn to get along with our neighbors and the people in town. This is going to be our home.'

'Yeah, we'll likely end up with a home six foot under ground,' Cory grumbled.

Dave shook his head. 'I'm beginning to worry some, Mom. Did I have a mouth as big at sixteen as Cory?'

'You were the man of the house at fourteen, what with your dad off fighting in the Indian campaigns.'

'And you're still the man of the house.' Adam spoke up at last, displaying a grin. ' 'Cause Cory and me together can't whip you . . . yet.'

'What is the plan for work today?' Mrs Kenyon got down to business.

'Cory and Adam need to continue building the fence up at the mouth of the canyon,' Dave answered. Then he regarded his brothers with a serious look. 'Keep a rifle close by at all times,' he warned. 'Those bandits might still be around.'

'You should have shot them all,' Adam said. 'If they were Angel Gervaso's men, they are a bunch of cold-blooded killers.'

'I'm not an executioner,' Dave replied. 'I can't shoot someone just because I think he might be a bandit or thief, Adam. If they had tried anything, I would have been forced to shoot. As it was, they dropped their guns and left without a fight.'

'Yeah, but what if they come back?' Cory asked.

'We'll deal with it when and if it happens.'

'You do as David says and keep your rifles handy,' Mrs Kenyon told the two younger Kenyon boys. 'If you see trouble coming, you get your horses and high-tail it for home. I don't want you trying to shoot it out with a band of killers.'

'Sure, Mom,' Cory said. 'We aren't going to start a war by ourselves.'

She accepted his promise and turned to Dave.

'Where will you be?'

'I'm going to see if I can round up a few head of wild cattle. If we drive them well up into the canyon, they should stay there until we finish the fence. With a little luck, we'll have a start on a sizable herd by the end of the month.'

'People are going to think we're crazy,' Cory groaned. 'Hardly anyone even shoots those stringy critters for meat . . . and we're going to make us a maverick herd.'

Dave didn't voice his agreement. There were reputed to be tens of thousands of wild longhorn cattle roaming free throughout Texas. Someone had given them the name of mavericks, as most of them were untamed and without brands, belonging to no one. His father had suggested they try and round some of them up into a herd. He seemed to think that when the price of beef got high enough back East there would be a market for even tough, lean, untamed cattle.

There was a box canyon beyond their ranch, one with both feed and a natural spring. With his two younger brothers working to construct a fence across the mouth of the canyon, they would soon have a place to hold and provide fodder for at least a hundred head of cattle. The real job was going to be catching or driving the wild beasts up into their makeshift pen.

'Your father told me there are some other men starting to put brands on maverick cattle,' Mrs Kenyon declared. 'He says we'll have to hurry, before someone else gets the same idea around here.'

'We'll make a sweep and gather as many as we can, once we get a place to hold them. There's only so much the three of us can do.'

'Do the best you can,' his mother said.

Dave turned to his brothers. 'Let's get going, guys.'

Cory continued to mutter, but he and Adam were soon gathering the supplies they needed to work on the fence. Dave saddled his horse, donned his riding-chaps and picked out his best rope. He was in the saddle by the time his brothers left the yard.

Mrs Kenyon came out, stopping him before he left.

'I spoke to Mrs Delton yesterday, David. She said they were expecting a shipment of supplies and goods for their store. Would you go by and see if they got in the salt and sugar she ordered? We're about out of both.'

'Sure, Mom.'

She moved over next to his horse and handed him some money.

'That should be plenty for what we need.'

'You need the stuff right away?'

'No, bring it home with you at quitting time.'

Dave gave a nod of understanding and lifted a hand in farewell. Then he put his horse toward town.

By mid-morning, Dave had already been to town and

was searching the foothills near the river. He knew many of the cattle came to water along that stretch. It had been his idea to gather several cattle at one time and try to drive them in a bunch.

He had stopped to rest his mount, when he heard something going through the brush. He turned in that direction and saw a streak of white moving swiftly. He started to reach for his rifle, but then a fleet-footed girl appeared, holding her dress up above her knees so she could run.

Dave recognized the flowing blonde mane, wild and bouncing with the girl's every step. He kicked his horse into motion and cut through the brush to head her off.

Jenny spotted him coming and waved frantically, turning in his direction. She was panting and completely winded when he pulled his horse to a stop a few feet in front of her.

'I saw . . .' she gulped in a swallow of air, 'I think I saw an Indian!' she gasped. 'Down by the creek!'

Dave swung his gaze off in that direction. 'He see you?'

She shook her head. 'No, I don't think so. I crept away, dropped my gathering basket and then ran. He's . . .' she gasped for air, still panting from the long sprint, 'back there . . .' she pointed, 'maybe a half-mile or so.'

'Was it a Comanche?'

'Excuse me!' She was indignant. 'But I didn't take time to check the cut of his clothing or the design of his war paint!'

'What are you doing so far away from home?'

'Our place is only a mile or so.' She defended herself. 'I was picking wild currants for jam. They are plentiful down along the creek.'

Dave would have liked to take a look for the Indian. If there was only one, he might be looking to steal a horse or some food. If there were several, it could mean an actual raid. However, he couldn't very well leave Jenny on foot and all alone.

'How come you're down this way?' the girl asked.

'I was scouting for maverick cattle. Pa has a mind for us to round up a few head and start a herd.'

'A herd of wild cattle?'

Dave shrugged his shoulders.

'There might come a time when those people back East get hungry enough to buy about any kind of beef.'

'If you say so.' She was doubtful. 'I would think rounding them up would be like trying to collect a herd of deer or elk.'

'They're about as wild,' he admitted. 'Climb up and I'll take you home.' As he made the offer, he kicked his foot free of the stirrup and stretched out a hand for the girl.

Jenny frowned at the offer.

'I think I might be safer with the Indians.'

'You can sit on back if you don't trust me,' he teased. 'That way, you can hang on to me . . . or the rawhide straps on the saddle, if you don't trust yourself.'

'Yeah, right,' she said drily. 'And if I sit in front, you'll have your arms around me!'

'It's your choice,' he said. 'What'll it be, Sparks?'

In spite of her anxiety and the remaining apprehension over meeting up with an Indian, Jenny
displayed the hint of a smile.

'I'll take the back seat.'

Dave took hold of her hand and, once she had her
left foot in the stirrup, he pulled her upward. She
swung her leg over the back of the horse and sprang
into place behind him and the saddle.

'You've ridden this way before,' he observed,
taking note of the ease of which she had gotten
aboard.

'Nester is the only horse we have,' she explained.
'We use him to pull the wagon, but he belongs to my
brother. My dad gave him to Kip for his birthday.'
She sobered a bit at the memory. 'It was the last time
we saw our father alive.'

Dave didn't wish to speak of the war and suffering,
so he kept the conversation focused.

'And Kip won't let you ride his horse?' he asked.

'Oh, he lets me ride all right . . . behind him, like
this.'

Dave put his gelding into an easy lope. He enjoyed
the way Jenny placed her hands on his waist to hang
on.

After a short way and an awkward silence, he
slowed his horse to a walk and spoke over his shoulder to Jenny. 'I went by the store this morning,
before I started my hunt down along the creek. They
got in a load of supplies at last. Been a real chore to
fix meals without either sugar or salt around the
house.'

'Yes, we've been robbing from our last pickle

65

barrel for salt and we've been out of sugar for several weeks. We use honey as a substitute, whenever Kip and I can locate honeycombs and steal it from the bees.'

'Makes for a bland diet,' Dave said.

'Pone and grits are pretty tasteless, even when you have something with which to flavor them.'

'I wonder if they'll have a run on the store and sell out?'

'It doesn't matter.' Jenny was subdued. 'The Deltons had to stop giving credit some time back and we don't have any cash money. We're raising some chickens to trade, but the chicks won't be fryer size for a while yet.'

Dave was all too aware of how his family was one of the few around who actually had money coming in. Texas was broke from the war. What money there was mostly belonged to the élite Union supporters or to the incoming carpetbaggers. Jobs, when a grown man could find one, was paid out at a few cents and a meal for a ten- or twelve-hour work day.

'I actually picked up twice as much as my mother asked,' Dave said carefully. 'I could let you have a couple pounds of each.'

'I told you, we don't have any money.'

Dave cocked his head, so he could look back over his shoulder. 'Maybe we could make a deal for it?'

A scowl came into Jenny's face. 'What kind of deal, Yank?'

'Gramps is having another dance over at his livery next Saturday night. Are you going?'

Gramps was a one-legged war veteran. He had

been sixty years old when the war started, yet he went to fight for the Confederacy. Ordinarily, a man his age would have been turned down, but he was something of an expert with black powder. His military career had not lasted long, courtesy of a Yankee cannon, which had nearly blown him to pieces. He owned the only livery in town and earned a living stabling horses and doing a little blacksmithing.

'Kip and I will probably go to the dance,' she admitted carefully, 'especially now that I have a new dress to show off.'

'I sure look forward to seeing you in it.'

'Yes, well, my mother would give birth to a cow if you were to ask me to dance. She still hates you Yanks.'

'One dance for a sack each of salt and sugar.' Dave made the offer. 'I'll take my chances on your mother not being real enthusiastic about the idea.'

'No.'

'Listen, Sparks,' he tried again, 'I wasn't in the fight at Vicksburg, where your father and brother were killed. We were on different sides, but I was never involved in any battles fought against the Texicans.'

'It makes no difference,' she argued. 'You're a Yankee. Ma will likely skin me alive if she finds out I've been riding on the back of your horse.'

'Yeah, but you're here,' he pointed out.

'Only to escape from a pack of bloodthirsty Indians!'

'I thought you didn't get a good look at the *one* Indian.'

Jenny uttered an unfeminine grunt.

'If my ma sees me ride up with you, I'm going to tell her there were at least a dozen renegades, all wearing war paint and hot on my trail!'

Dave made a turn on to the lane which led to the Moran farm. Jenny took notice of the change in direction and a question came to mind.

'I never asked you, when you showed up at my house last time. How did you know where I lived?'

'I figure it's about time I started courting, Sparks. I've been in Three Forks long enough to know where all of the pretty girls live.'

'Oh, yeah?' she challenged. 'So how many girls are on your list for courting?'

'You want the truth?'

'Yes?'

'You mean, how many girls, counting all of the pretty girls around Three Forks, including the nearby farms and ranches?'

'Yes,' she said again.

'And counting you as one of them?'

'Yes!' she snapped, angry at his delay in answering, 'counting me!'

He snickered under his breath, then stated: 'One.'

Dave felt the girl's grip tighten ever so slightly at the news.

'Just me?' she asked, her voice suddenly hesitant and sounding a little uncertain.

'Just you, Sparks,' he admitted. 'I reckon you're the sweetest, prettiest, most charming girl in these parts. Pa always said I should aim high and go for the best.'

'If my pa was around, I'm sure he'd aim high too. He'd likely aim about as high as your cold, black heart!'

The Moran house came into sight, so Dave swung off the trail and into the nearby brush to remain out of sight. When he stopped, Jenny was already sliding over the back of the horse.

'You shouldn't dismount that way,' he scolded her. 'What if this horse was a little green? He might have kicked you.'

'He didn't,' she said simply. Then she came around to face him. She had to use a hand to shield her eyes from the overhead sun. 'Thank you for the rescue . . . again.'

Dave reached into the sack he had tied to the front of his saddle and removed two small packages. Before Jenny could say anything to stop him, he passed them down to her.

She caught each packet, but gave a negative shake of her head.

'I can't take these!'

'One dance Saturday night,' Dave repeated his offer. 'You can't tell me a couple pounds of salt and sugar isn't worth three or four minutes of kicking some straw around to music.'

Jenny stared at the packages as if trying to decide how to either keep them or give them back. He decided to use her spirited disposition to win his point.

'Maybe you're afraid of what people might say?' he suggested, displaying a cryptic simper. 'I can under-stand your being intimidated by the other folks

69

around town – especially Rex Jardeen.'

'I'm not afraid of what people think,' she retorted, 'least of all Rex! But my mother has a quick hand and a short fuse. She'll knock me a good one if she hears I danced with a Yankee.'

'Tell her I demanded payment for saving you from a bunch of wild savages.'

'To my ma's way of thinking, you and your family are no better than wild savages!'

He grinned and touched the tip of his worn, flat-crowned, wide-brimmed hat in a polite gesture.

'The stuff is yours to keep, Sparks,' he said. 'If you don't want to make it right by dancing with me, that's fine.'

'It's not fine!' she snapped. 'We Morans don't take no charity. We always pay for what we get!'

'Good,' he said smugly. 'Then I look forward to seeing you Saturday night.'

'Yes . . .' Jenny still appeared uncertain, 'I might see you . . . but I ain't agreeing that I'll dance with you.'

Rather than spend any more time arguing, Dave lifted a hand in farewell. Then he swung his horse about and started up the trail. He had to get back and have a look at those Indians. His ranch was close enough to be a target. He dared not continue his visit with Jenny when he could possibly avert or thwart a Comanche raid.

Grace Moran looked much older than her forty-three years. Her hair had streaks of gray and there were age lines around her eyes, creasing her forehead and camped at the corners of her mouth. She seldom smiled, having grown weary and despondent after the deaths of her husband and elder son.

Jenny entered the house to discover her mother busy mashing a bowl of potatoes. She had a couple of jars nearby on the table. Jenny knew she would put the mashed potatoes, along with some of their precious salt and some dried honey into a jar. Next, she would add a little warm water and set them on a shelf. After two days, covered with a cloth, the concoction would ferment and produce a portion of yeast, which was needed to bake bread.

'You're back early,' the woman remarked, looking up from her work. 'Did you already fill your basket with berries?'

'I-I'm sorry, mother. I left the basket down by the river.' She was hesitant about how much she should say. 'I saw an Indian and ran for my life.'

The woman ceased working at once and came around the table to examine Jenny from head to foot.

'He didn't hurt you?'

'I'm pretty sure he didn't even see me,' she answered. 'I . . . I ran until I chanced upon a neighbor. He gave me a ride home.'

'A neighbor?' A sudden suspicion clouded the woman's face. 'Which neighbor?'

'Well, I suppose he's closer to being a stranger than a neighbor.' Jenny corrected herself. 'But I know he's a good shot with a rifle.' She continued to avoid a direct answer.

'Jennifer Faye Moran, who was the neighbor?' her

mother demanded to know.

It made no sense to hide the truth.

'The same one who saved me and Kip from those three ruffians the other day,' she admitted at last.

The woman clenched her teeth together and a red hue stained her cheeks.

'Not that blasted Yankee again!'

'Dave Kenyon was searching for wild longhorn cattle. He said their family was going to start a herd.'

'A herd of those wild beasts?' She laughed her disdain. 'And you think he isn't as dumb as a tree-stump!'

'He gave us these,' Jenny confessed, stepping over to place the salt and sugar on the table. 'He said the store only got in a small amount, so he picked up some extra.'

'Charity?' she wailed. 'You're taking charity from a Yank?'

'No. I traded him for it.'

'Traded what?' her mother demanded to know.

'Uh,' she had no ready reply, 'just something he wanted.'

Her mother's scowl was enough to frost a lighted candle.

'What do we have that a low-down Yankee would want?'

Jenny knew it was a waste of time to try and deceive her mother.

'He traded it for a dance with me Saturday night.'

Rather than blowing up and spouting a string of unladylike words, her mother reached out and fingered the two bags.

'Sugar and salt,' she said, her anger melting into a grave sadness. 'My daughter is selling her favors for a couple pounds of sugar and salt.'

'I'm not selling my favors!' Jenny defended her honor. 'There's a good chance I would have danced with him anyway – without taking any bribe. He tried to give us the sugar and salt because he wanted to be nice. When I wouldn't take it, he said he would trade the stuff for a dance.'

'It sure sounds like he's paying for your favors.'

'I'm sorry if you feel that way, Mother,' Jenny said. 'But I'm not going to duck my head in shame for dancing with David Kenyon, not when he saved me and Kip from those bandits. He has been nothing but a proper gentleman!'

Her mother continued to glower.

'What about Mrs Kenyon?' Jenny turned the challenge toward her. 'You've seen her at the church meetings on Sunday. Do you think of her as a no-good Yankee?'

'She volunteers for every charity that comes along,' her mother acknowledged. 'And she even brought some honey rolls to pass around last week.' She lowered her head. 'I'm ashamed to admit I ate one . . . without even thinking of saving it to share with you kids.'

'Eating a honey roll doesn't make you a traitor to our family, Mother,' Jenny replied. 'And my taking a little salt and sugar doesn't mean I'm selling my favors to a Yank.'

'It's so hard to forget the war . . . what with your father and brother gone.'

'And it's no fault of David Kenyon's that he fought with the Yanks,' Jenny argued. 'He joined to fight because his father was already serving in the Union army. He told me he wasn't involved in the battle at Vicksburg – and I believe him.'

'Your brother had just become a man when he went off with your father!' Grace reminded her hotly. 'And some blasted Yank shot and killed him!'

Jenny emitted a sigh.

'I don't wish to fight with you, Mother. You can throw out the sugar and salt, if you want, but I'm not going to take it back.'

'First, the Yank buys you a new dress. Now he's making a deal to force you to dance with him. I worry where this is heading.'

'It's heading nowhere, Mother,' she said with some resolution. 'If David shows up at the dance Saturday, I'll give him his one dance. Then we'll be even.'

'Yes . . .' The woman surrendered to Jenny's logic. 'You'll be even.'

CHAPTER SIX

The shadowy figure was moving too fast for stealth. He stepped on a stick, which cracked loudly underfoot, then cursed a thorny wild rose which caught hold of his sleeve and scratched his arm. He moved recklessly, threading his way through the trees at a near run. Dave had seen a few Indians before and they moved like ghosts. This man was like a bull going through a cornfield. After a glimpse or two, he was certain the man in the brush was no Indian.

Leaving his horse tethered where he could munch a little bunch grass, Dave took his rifle and set off in a direction to intercept the unknown visitor. He had done enough hunting to know how to avoid making noise. He used the high brush to hide his movements and angled ahead of the intruder. Then he took up a position behind a rock and waited for the man to show himself.

The fellow soon appeared on the trail. It was easy to see why Sparks had thought he was an Indian. He had the appearance of an Apache, dressed in linen trousers and shirt, with his evenly cropped, shoulder-length black hair held in place with a cloth head-band. He was obviously in a hurry, jogging along at a good clip. Curiously, he appeared more interested in keeping watch over his back trail than looking where he was going. It allowed Dave a chance to catch him out in the open, not fifty feet from his position.

'*Alto*!' he ordered, then stepped out from behind his cover. 'Stop!'

The young man skidded to a halt and raised his hands. Dave could see he was not armed, not even a knife.

'Do you *habla* English? Can you talk our tongue?' Dave asked, keeping the man under the muzzle of his rifle.

'From the sounds of it,' the youth answered smartly, 'a lot better than you.'

Dave lowered his rifle and approached warily. 'You're not Indian.' It was a statement.

'Mexican,' the boy replied.

'Where did you come from?'

'I hail from the village of Rio Blanco, fifty miles or so across the border. I am a student of Padre Jordan Powell. He has a mission there.'

'So, kid, what are you doing here?'

'Name's Rico Valdez . . . or as the padre calls me – Ricky.'

'OK, Ricky. I'm Dave Kenyon. What brings you to our side of the river?'

'The bandit leader, Angel Gervaso.'

Dave approached to stand before the young man. He appeared to be in late adolescence, with an alert intelligence shining in his eyes. Shorter by six inches than Dave, he was stockily built and looked very fit.

'You hungry?' Dave asked. 'I've got some jerky and hard rolls on my horse.'

'It's been a while since I ate,' Ricky admitted.

Dave led the way, not asking any questions. He knew the fellow would eventually tell him why he had come. The fact that he had news about Gervaso was disturbing, but he would wait until the information was offered.

Once back by his horse, he dug out his lunch and shared it with the young Mexican. Ricky took what was offered and they ate in silence. Dave guessed, considering the young man's excellent command of English, that the padre might have raised or influenced the boy for a good many years.

After passing over his canteen so that the youth could drink, Dave sat back and waited for him to spill his story.

'There was a wild party in town the other night,' the boy began. 'I was listening to the music and watching the girls dance.' Now he grew serious. 'Several of Gervaso's men arrived and they began to drink and dance with some of the *señoritas*. They usually mind their manners around Rio Blanco, because they often make camp near there. They even pay for the supplies and goods they get.

'Anyway, I overheard them talking about a settlement they were going to pillage in the next day or two.' He put steady eyes on Dave. 'One of them mentioned Three Forks.'

'So you came to warn us?'

'I told the padre, but there are no able men at the

mission, only women and children and those too old to get around on their own. It was agreed that I should come and alert you folks to the danger.'

'I had a run-in with three bandit sorts the other day,' Dave informed him. 'I was afraid they might belong to Angel Gervaso. It appears they were looking us over to see if we would make an easy next victim.'

'I'll stay and help you fight them,' Ricky offered.

'Why should you do that?'

'Gervaso rides bold and in the open now, with thirty riders at his side. It was not always so. As a mere bandit, he had only a few men, but they were ruthless and cruel. When they attacked a small village or trading post, they killed anyone who stood against them. Soon the people learned to run and hide from them.

'My village had not heard of Angel Gervaso. When he attacked, my family did not know of his brutality.' He lifted a hand and pushed back the hair near his right temple. It revealed a whitish scar. 'One of them shot me as I ran for a weapon. He was confident of his skill and thought he had killed me.' Ricky took a deep breath and let it out slowly. His face was dark and somber at the memory. 'When I awoke, Gervaso's men had killed several in our village, and everyone else had run to hide in the hills. In all, there were nine people shot and seven of them died. I was the only one who survived from my family.'

'I'm sorry,' Dave told him.

'If the padre had not taken me in, I would have probably starved to death. He taught me English, so that I might help him teach the other children. We have mostly orphans and widows at the mission.'

'And so you came to warn us and save us from the same fate as your family suffered?'

'Yes,' he said, displaying a grim determination, 'and to help put an end to Gervaso and his murderous raids.'

'Can you shoot?'

'There are ways to fight without being able to shoot,' he replied. 'I can help.'

'We'll get everyone together for a town meeting tonight. Do you know when they might attack Three Forks?'

'In a day or two, from the way they talked.'

'Let's get my horse and get going. I'll need to send word to all of the nearby farms and ranches too.'

The only place large enough for a town meeting was at Gramps's barn. He had some wooden benches, which were used for Sunday meetings and placed along the walls for the monthly dance. For the emergency meeting, he had placed them in rows and the place was crowded.

Gramps took charge, gray and bent with his years, hobbling on his one good leg, while using a cane to help shuffle his useless limb. He wore his gray Rebel cap and had a gun on his hip. The pistol butt was what he used to pound on the preaching-pulpit to get everyone's attention.

'Quiet down!' he ordered. 'This here meeting be in order!'

Once the women had quieted the kids and the others were silent, Gramps looked over the gathering.

'This here Yank,' he bobbed his head at Dave, 'he come on to Ricky Valdez down by the river today. Ricky is a young gent from the Mexican village of Rio Blanco.' He regarded those who had gathered with a stern look. 'Ricky says Angel Gervaso is headed our way.'

Fear leapt into the faces of the women and dread and apprehension swept over everyone in attendance.

'You all know what them scoundrels done over at Gloryville,' Gramps continued. 'Them folks didn't put up any fight at all, yet Gervaso's bunch burned the place to the ground.'

'How do we know we can trust a Yank and some wandering Mexican?' Rex Jardeen asked. 'What if this is some kind of prank?' He glared at Dave. 'We all know how the Yanks like to play dirty tricks.'

Dave groaned at the stupidity of the remark. He wondered if Rex had heard about the episode with the bandits and Jenny. If so, he might be letting jealousy affect his thinking.

'Why would we make up a story like that?' Dave kept his outward calm. 'What would we have to gain by frightening the entire town?'

'I overheard Gervaso's men talking.' Ricky spoke up, addressing the group. 'They spoke of Three Forks and said how it would be easy pickings, because there were few men here who could fight.'

His words were met with shouts and questions. Everyone wanted answers at the same time. Gramps eventually banged his gun butt on the tabletop for silence again.

'All right!' he said, looking over the sea of anxious faces. 'We got trouble headed our way. The only question is, what do we do about it?'

For a few seconds, no one spoke. Then Dave took the floor.

'If we can get someone to a telegraph office we can send for help from the Union troops. My father will see to it that we get a company of men down here to stop Gervaso.'

Several called out jeers or made snide remarks about the Yankees being responsible for men like Gervaso. Rex shouted that the Yankees could go to hell and others nodded their agreement. Gramps kept a cooler head. He lifted a hand to quieten the crowd once more.

'You people all know me,' he began. 'I was making fireworks for the Fourth of July celebration by the time I was knee-high to a piano stool. I've been a part of this town since it was settled some twenty years ago. I fought against the Mexican army with Sam Houston himself, back when Texas won her independence.'

He paused to rest his gaze on Dave's family. 'And I was wounded at Chickamauga in sixty-three, after I had joined up with the Confederate army of Tennessee. Reason I went all the way to Tennessee is because I had met and liked those boys, back when they come to help in Texas during our own little war.' He sighed and his shoulders sagged. 'I seen the worst of the Yanks in battle,' he said. 'But I tell you, they were no different from the rest of us. They fought bravely and died like men.' He snorted. 'Them on

81

the field were not like these bloodsucking, blue-belly, riff-raff they sent to Texas to enforce their military law. These are the worst of any army lot. They ain't real soldiers, they are occupation troops.'

He gave a nod at the Kenyon family.

'Nonetheless, Captain Will Kenyon was one of them decent fighting Yanks, a soldier with near twenty years in the army. I only talked to him a couple times, but I know he ain't in favor of the Union standing with its heel on our necks. I agree with his boy. If we can get word to him, he'll send help.'

'It's seventy miles to Adobe Flats and the nearest telegraph office.' One of the few men in the room spoke up. 'The stage won't be through for two weeks, so we can't send for help though the mail.'

'And Gervaso might already have the town under surveillance.' The man's wife was quick to take his side. 'What if they are also watching, in case we try and get a message out? They might kill our messenger.'

The words caused more rumbling through the group. There were real concerns about Gervaso's band of cut-throats. Word had spread how his men had already been in the valley and one had died harassing Kip and Jenny Moran. Anyone trying to leave might be stopped or even killed.

'No one will think I am one of you.' Ricky spoke up. 'Who will pay special attention to a lone Mexican?'

'Only every renegade Indian for miles around or anyone with a grudge against the Mexicans.' Dave spoke up.

'Someone has to go,' Ricky argued. 'I've never shot a gun, but I can ride a horse.'

'I'll go with him.' Kip was the one to speak up. 'I know the way. We can stick to the hills until after we get well away from town, then make a run for Adobe Flats.'

Mrs Moran was alarmed at the idea.

'No! I can't let you do it, Kip!'

'He might be volunteering for the safest chore.' Rex spoke up again. 'If Gervaso's bunch shows up in the next couple days, we won't have a prayer. Even if Kip and the Mexican get through, Yankee troops won't reach us for four or five days. The town might be nothing but a pile of cold ashes by then.'

Ricky again took the floor. 'It sounded to me like Gervaso was not coming himself.' He told the gathering. 'From what I managed to overhear from the loose talk, it sounded as if they were only sending a handful of men here to Three Forks. They don't feel you have enough guns to oppose them.'

'Any idea how many?' Dave asked the question.

'I didn't hear an actual number, but they were speaking of splitting up into several groups. My guess would be no more than eight or ten.'

'Even that many would be tough for us to handle,' Rex said. 'Look around! We've only got four healthy men in town, plus a half-dozen boys not yet twenty years old. Add Gramps and a couple cripples from the war and it sure ain't much of an army.'

'I can shoot as well as you, Rex,' Jenny spoke up. 'So can my mother.'

'You ain't in no danger out at your farm,' Rex argued. 'It's the town they are going to hit.'

'It's our town too!' Jenny fired back.

The declaration encouraged a number of others to sound off. Gramps finally had to pound the table to quieten the group.

'I'm for counting heads and putting this here to a vote,' he said. Then he paused to look over at the Kenyon family, gradually moving his gaze to the farmers and the other small ranchers. 'Rex told it straight,' he went on, 'them what don't live here in town would likely not have to worry about being attacked. That means you needn't vote to fight, unless you want to throw in with us to defend the town.' Then he allowed for everyone to have a moment to think. Eventually, he looked over the group again.

'Let's see the hands,' he declared. 'How many of you want to let those men take what they want? We do nothing but sit back and not get in the way of Gervaso's thugs?'

One timid hand started upward, then it was retracted back at once.

Gramps gave a nod. 'OK, so how many of you intend to put up a fight?'

Rex rose up quickly. 'One thing, before you lift your hands,' he warned the gathering. 'It's worth mentioning how Gervaso's men handled the people in Gloryville. A couple died from being roughed up, but there was no outright killing. If we choose to fight and injure or kill some of his men, he will want us all dead.'

84

'One of his men is already dead,' Kip reminded Rex. 'Kenyon shot a man named Juan Gervaso, likely a relative to Angel. The *comancheros* might be figuring on a little revenge, no matter what we do . . . or don't do.'

'Good thinking, Kenyon.' Rex growled his words. 'We needed Gervaso to have a personal grudge against us.'

'He killed that man for my sake!' Jenny spoke up, glaring at Red. 'He could have sat back and let them do whatever they wanted, but he didn't. He saved me from harm or maybe even death. Don't you dare start blaming him for this mess!'

Rex shrank back, emotionally slapped down from her heated retort. Tom Delton used the momentary silence to raise his own voice.

'There are two ways to handle men like Gervaso. We either stand and fight, or we evacuate the town and let them take everything of value. If we choose the latter, we will have to hope they don't set fire to every building when they leave. Gramps is right about the choice, we can cower and run or fight and maybe die.'

The gravity of his words hit home. These were hardworking families, few with able-bodied men left in their family. Of the four men in the room, only one had fought in the war. The other three had either been too young when the war started or they had been left behind by fathers and brothers to act as heads of their family. Two were newly married and were struggling to put food on the table. If they were killed, who would look after their new households?

'No one younger than fourteen is to vote,' Gramps

warned. He took another breath, so the words could sink in. He pointed at Ricky and Kip. 'You two already voted to ride for help, so you don't need to raise your hands.' Then he swept over the group with his flinty eyes. 'All right, let's see the hands of them that wish to fight.'

Dave's hand went up at the same time as Jenny's. He caught her glance and flashed her a grim smile. She looked away quickly, embarrassed he had caught her looking in his direction.

Around the room, every eligible hand was lifted. No one was willing to sit back and be victimized by Gervaso's men. They had all voted to fight.

Shortly after daylight, Ricky and Kip were fitted out with two of the finest riding-horses at the stable and provided with supplies enough for three days. Gramps checked directions with the boys, then Mrs Moran spoke a soft goodbye to Kip and hugged him.

'You're not yet men in the eyes of the world,' Gramps told the two, after they had mounted their horses, 'but you're both men in our hearts. Once we make our stand against his gang, Angel Gervaso is likely to come here with his full force. We're counting on you to get help back here before he arrives to wipe us out.'

'We'll get word to the army,' Kip vowed.

'If need be, send off a wire to Captain Will Kenyon at El Paso. Even if he can't reach us in time to stop Gervaso himself, I'm sure he will get some troops headed this way.'

'Don't worry about us, Gramps,' Kip said. 'We'll

get help back as soon as we can.'

'Good luck, boys.'

Kip lifted a hand in farewell, then waved at his mother and Jenny, who were watching from a short way off. Jenny showed him a supportive smile and waved in return. Then the two boys were riding through the alley and up into the nearby foothills. Even if someone was keeping watch over the town, it was unlikely they would spot the pair.

As soon as Kip and Ricky had left Gramps called together the war council. Dave Kenyon was no longer a Yank, he was one of the defenders of the town. He and the other men had spent most of the night outlining a battle-plan.

The group comprised Gramps, four married men, Rex and Dave, plus nine boys and six girls over the age of fourteen. There were also three women and a couple cripples from the war. They constituted the bulk of the Three Forks fighting force.

'Way I see it,' Gramps outlined for the group, 'we need to capture or turn back Angel Gervaso's men – if possible, without killing any of them.'

'You're the fireworks man.' Tom Delton spoke up. 'How can we do that?'

'First off, we need to devise a warning so we will know his men are on their way.' He tipped his head toward Dave.

'Our place is not far from the main trail,' Dave told the others. 'My two younger brothers will keep watch during the day. We don't figure Gervaso's boys will be worried about any trap or ambush, as they don't know we have been warned.'

'How do your brothers get word to us?' a woman asked.

'They will send up a smoke signal when they spot Gervaso's men,' Dave answered. 'Gramps gave me a handful of sulfur and yellow dye. My brothers only have to start a fire and dump the powder into the flames. It will put up a yellow smoke that we can see from town.'

'We'll have some of the younger kids around town watching for the smoke signal,' Gramps informed the group.

'You say we don't want any of the raiders killed.' Rex spoke up. 'How do we stop them?'

Gramps picked up a couple pieces of paper.

'Several of us spent the night working over some ideas. We'll form up into teams and set our trap. I'll keep the ladies here to help me prepare some fireworks. Each of the older men will be in charge of several of the younger people. We need to get started right away. No telling how much time we have.'

Rex was doubtful. 'I don't see us being able to capture or run off a bunch of killers with only the use of some smoke and Fourth of July fireworks.'

'Dave Kenyon, Ben Stokes and Jenny Moran,' Tom Delton spoke up, 'you are with me.'

The other three men all followed suit, announcing the names of those people who were to work with them. Rex glowered at Dave, obviously thinking he had something to do with Jenny being chosen to work on his team. Dave was forced to hide a smile, because he *had* helped assign the teams!

Jenny waited until they were out of the barn

before she also put a curious gaze on Dave.

'How do you think I was so fortunate as to be in your little group?'

'What can I say, Sparks? It must be fate.'

'Sure, like I believe that.'

Tom stopped at the corral.

'Dave, you ride out and get your brothers lined out for keeping watch,' he directed. 'Then you meet us at the big hanging-tree at the edge of town. I'll climb the tree and we'll start stringing the wire for our fly-trap.'

'I'll pick up the needed surprise on my way back,' Dave told him.

'You sure you can handle it alone?'

'I know where to find it,' Dave replied. 'I'll have my brothers' help, before I have them start their watches.'

Tom grinned. 'If this works, it ought to make for a lively reception.'

Jenny frowned from one man to the other.

'Whatever are you talking about?'

'You'll see,' Tom told her. 'It's one of the treats we're going to prepare for Gervaso's boys.'

Dave headed for his horse. 'I'll see you all back here in a couple hours.'

Jenny might have asked further questions, but Tom walked away, leading her and Ben toward the general store to gather a few supplies.

CHAPTER SEVEN

Fryer kicked dirt over the last embers of the morning fire. He stopped to glance up at the sun. 'We should have been in the saddle two hours ago, Pudge.'

Pudge stretched his arms, still reclined on his ground blanket.

'There's no big rush, my friend. Three Forks is not going anywhere.'

'If Gervaso was here he'd have kicked your tail out of bed at first light.'

'What can I say? I'm not the tyrant he is. We rode hard yesterday. The horses needed a little extra rest and it felt good to sleep late.'

'We'll have to spend the next fifteen hours in the saddle if we are to reach Three Forks before nightfall.'

'You worry too much, Fryer. We'll camp a few miles from town tonight. That way, we can ride into town tomorrow morning. No need having to rush our visit and maybe miss something of value. We can take our time and ransack each house or store at our leisure. We'll finish early, fire the buildings and be able to get a good start on our return. By the time word reaches the army about the raid, we'll be half-way back to the border.'

Fryer grinned. 'Maybe we ought to let the boys have an election as to our leader. You are definitely easier to work for than El Gervaso.'

'In all sorts of ways, Fryer,' Pudge said, laughing. 'I won't even stop you men from bringing along a few of the *señoritas* or kids for us to sell or ransom.'

'Gervaso will like that, Pudge. We haven't taken any hostages for several months.'

'It will take the American army weeks to get permission to cross into Mexico,' Pudge replied. 'It will be less expensive for them to pay for the return of those we take.'

'Good thinking,' Fryer agreed.

'We missed our chance on the last raid,' Pudge grumbled. 'We should have done the same thing at Gloryville.'

'It looks like Keen and Chico have the horses saddled,' Fryer told Pudge. 'And Red is about done packing the supplies on the mule.'

'I guess that means we're ready to move out.' Pudge found his hat. He checked to see no insects had taken up residence before placing it on his head. Then he rose to his feet.

Fryer stood close enough for only Pudge to be able to hear his words.

'I would feel better if we had more men. Five of us to take on a whole town isn't very good odds.'

'The people of Three Forks will have heard about Gloryville,' Pudge reminded him. 'They will be too afraid to stand up to us.'

'If you say so.'

'You will see, my friend. These people will scatter and run like fieldmice from the harrow. They will see five tough, armed men, ready to kill and slaughter them to the last person, and they will throw their hands in the air to surrender. I expect they will plead with us to take only their money, food and belongings . . . so long as we leave them their miserable lives.'

'You remember the man who put a bullet through my hat?' Fryer reminded him. 'What if he has friends who will fight too?'

'He probably wasn't even from the town of Three Forks,' Pudge suggested. 'We were several miles into the hills when we stopped the wagon. He was likely a *vaquero* or farmer, one who seldom goes into Three Forks. I don't think we'll have to worry about him.'

'I hope you're right.'

'You'll see, Fryer, my friend. We will ride into town like kings and those submissive weaklings will fall down on their knees before us.'

Fryer grinned at the thought.

'Then we strip the town bare.'

'We'll take everything of value . . . and Gervaso will praise us for our work.'

'I'm going to keep an eye out for that little gal we stopped on the trail,' Fryer announced. 'She still owes us each a kiss.'

'Yeah.' Pudge smiled at the memory. 'If you spot her, I'll be at your side – to get the kiss she owes me too!'

*

The young Ben Stokes etched out a narrow furrow with the pickax, marking a trail some two or three inches in depth. Jenny followed after him, unwinding twine from a ball and placing the strand in the bottom of the furrow. Then she would cover it over and pat the dirt back into place, burying the string. Ben was able to move much faster than she, so he was a hundred feet or so ahead of her when Rex Jardeen appeared.

'Where's the Yank?' Rex asked.

'He isn't back from his place yet. He had to stop and pick something up for our trap.'

'I don't like the idea of you two working together,' Rex snarled. 'It makes it look like you've taken up with him.'

Jenny paused from her hands and knees to glare up at him.

'I'm not taking up with anyone, Rex. I was assigned to Tom's team. I'm doing my share of the work.'

'I've seen the way that Yank looks at you,' Rex continued to rant. 'He's done everything but stake a claim for you!'

Jenny dropped the spool of twine and sprang up on to her feet.

'Don't you be talking to me like I'm a piece of property, Rex!' She placed her hands on her hips and glared at him in defiance. 'I've never said I was your girl.'

'You used to think it wasn't such a bad idea!' He threw the challenge back at her. 'I didn't see you trying to get away from me at the last barn dance. We spent the whole night dancing together.'

'Other than Dave Kenyon, you're about the only eligible guy around Three Forks who isn't married,' Jenny replied. 'It's not like there were a lot of men in line to pat you on the shoulder and cut in.'

'Yeah, I see how it is,' he sneered. 'You like the idea of having the Yank panting at your heels.'

Jenny gave her head a negative shake.

'This is a stupid conversation, Rex. My mother has not even allowed that I can talk to Dave Kenyon. If you want to get jealous, you'll have to wait until I'm actually seeing someone else.'

'Jealous?' He was imprudent. 'Why should I be jealous of some blue-belly scum?'

Jenny felt the fires of her anger surface.

'You best get back to your assigned chores, Rex!' she fumed. 'You're on the verge of forcing me to defend a Yankee, and I would darn well despise you for that!'

Rex was surprised at the intensity behind her words. It caused him to take a step back.

'Sure.' He cowed, quick to try and make amends. 'I didn't mean for you to get upset, Jenny.'

'So leave me alone!'

Ben heard her last words, as he had finished digging the line to the edge of the corral. He moved forward, until he was standing a few feet from both Rex and Jenny.

'Is anything wrong?' he asked quietly.

'Stay out of this, Stokes!' Rex snarled at him. 'This ain't none of your business!'

'Don't be biting his head off!' Jenny hissed the

words at Rex. 'You're the one who is making a fuss over nothing!'

Rex doubled his fists impotently, his face grew red with his rage and he glowered at her.

'You call it nothing,' he snipped off the words curtly, 'but you've taken sides against me and your own town, Jenny. You've become a Yankee-lover! I hope you have a single friend when this is all over!' Then he spun on his heels and strode away, his head held high with an arrogant lift.

'Maybe you ought to save some of your fight for Gervaso's men!' Jenny called after him. 'You're going to need it!'

Ben waited in awkward silence until Jenny had taken her eyes off Rex. He recognized she was still steamed, so he didn't say anything about the encounter. Instead, he went around and hunkered down next to the miniature trench.

'You run the twine and I'll cover it,' he offered. 'I'm guessing it's pretty hard for you to crawl around in a dress.'

Jenny summoned her aplomb and returned to the chore at hand.

'Thanks, Ben,' she said. 'I'm glad someone around here is a gentleman.'

He smiled. 'I do believe that's the first time a girl ever called me a gentleman. I wonder what my ma would think about that.'

Jenny laughed. 'I'll tell her next time I see her.'

Ben got down on his hands and knees and began to push dirt over the twine.

'Get to running string,' he said. 'When you reach

the end, you can work back to me.'

Jenny began backing up a step at a time, unwinding the thick string and placing it in the furrow, so Ben could cover it over. They worked together, while Tom was busy positioning the cord along an overhanging limb on the tree. All they needed for their trap was Dave's surprise.

There could be no smoke signal as a warning after dark, so a guard was stationed fifty yards up the main road to keep watch. El Gervaso's men would be unlikely to know they had been forewarned, so there was little reason to suspect they would attempt to sneak into Three Forks. The raiders would likely be confident of their force, expecting no resistance from only a handful of men. Even so, the defenders of the town were taking no chances.

Dave was to maintain his vigil until midnight, when another man would come out to relieve him. He sat on the remains of a tree stump, one which had mostly been cut up and hauled off for firewood. The stump was about eight feet around and ten feet long, with a tangle of massive roots half-out of the ground. He was poised with his rifle across his lap, while he listened to the sounds of the night. Crickets chirped and there was an owl nearby that felt compelled to hoot every few minutes. Otherwise, it was quiet.

Then the sound of someone's light step turned his head. In the dim glow of the light from the half-moon, he saw the shadow of a person in a dress.

'Over here,' he said softly.

Jenny Moran moved from the middle of the road

and walked his direction. She picked him out of the shadows and came to stand next to him. He could see she was carrying something in her hands.

'I brought you some lemonade and cookies,' she said. 'My mother makes the best cookies in the country.'

'Sounds good. I haven't had any cookies for a spell.'

'She hasn't been able to make any lately, not until some thoughtful person gave us some sugar.'

He smiled. 'It's real thoughtful of you both. Pull up a tree-stump and sit down.'

Jenny turned around, swept the material of her dress until it was smooth with her free hand and took a seat on the tree next to him. Then she handed him two cookies.

Dave immediately took a bite out of one of them. The pastry was sweet and still warm.

'Ummm,' he gave his approval. 'These are good.'

'My father used to say he married Mother because of her cooking.' She smiled at the memory. 'And Mother liked to say she married him because he was rich.'

'Rich, huh?'

'He had his own horse, a wagon and thirty dollars when they got married. That's pretty rich, isn't it?'

Dave chuckled. 'Yeah, I'd call that being right well off.'

'How about your folks?'

'My pa was a corporal in the army, but he had a steady income – about six dollars a month. He was a master sergeant by the time the war began. When his commander was killed, he was given a field commission and became a lieutenant. With so many officers being lost in the fighting, he was soon promoted to captain and given his own company.' He chewed another mouthful of the pastry before he continued. 'He really hates the work here. A good many of the troops are rowdy and undisciplined. Most of the men stationed in Texas didn't fight in the war. They don't have a respect for the people or the ideals for which the Texicans were fighting.'

'You mean slavery?'

He gave his head a negative shake. 'Not only slavery, but more the political side of the war.'

'The political side?'

'The Southern or ultra-slavery Democrats demanded recognition of their party by the Northern Republicans and conservative Democrats. They declared that Congress should preserve their rights . . . including their sanction of slavery. Even President Lincoln, in his inaugural address, stated he had neither the right nor the desire to interfere with slavery where it already existed; but he refused to allow any state to withdraw from the Union. The Southern states wished to govern themselves and live under their own rule. Such a division would have destroyed both our country and our Constitution.'

'We never heard much of anything about the politics behind the war,' Jenny admitted.

'I'm sure most of the half-million men who died didn't know all of the reasons either,' Dave replied. 'Most men rallied to fight for their home state, unaware of the political objectives behind the war.'

'Mom said there was an item in the newspaper that stated one-third of the men from Texas were killed or wounded in the fighting.' She sighed deeply. 'It was an even higher ratio here in Three Forks.'

Dave nodded his agreement. 'The wounds and losses will take a long time to heal.'

'Especially while you Yanks continue to advocate martial law and the bullying of us Texicans.'

'Yes,' he agreed. 'That certainly doesn't help.'

Jenny was silent for a time while Dave finished off the second cookie. Then he downed a few swallows from the glass of lemonade.

'I can't see the surprise you brought to hang in the tree,' she said, looking up into the nearby branches.

'It's there, hidden by the darkness.'

'It must have been a chore, bringing something like that all the way to town.'

'Yes, it took me and my brothers about an hour. We used a lot of smoke and a thick canvas bag. The hard part was rigging the trip wire, so it will fall when we pull the twine.'

'Do you think this plan will work?'

Dave gave his shoulders a shrug. 'We've got trenches in place and soaked with coal-oil. We have hidden wire and ropes for the trap, plus Gramps has his toys set up and ready to go. If those fellows come in on the main trail, I think we'll give them a shock or two. We might get lucky and catch them all.'

'Then what?'

'We hold them for the authorities and hope my father gets us help before Angel Gervaso can send more men or come himself.'

'It's scary to think about what's ahead.'

'Yeah, Sparks, we've got a war all our own.'

'I hope my mother never hears you call me by that name. She'll demand to know why you are calling me Sparks!'

'If your mother is anything like you, she won't have to ask.'

'Thanks for your opinion,' she said sourly. 'That puts all of my concerns to rest.'

'You ought to be getting back within the confines of town,' he suggested, finishing the last sip of lemonade from the container. 'If Gervaso's men were to sneak up on the town, you might be caught out here with me.'

'Gervaso's men don't frighten me,' she quipped. 'My first concern is that my mother doesn't catch me out here with *you*.'

'She doesn't know?'

'I kind of sneaked away without telling her.'

'You are a bold little nymph.'

'Nymph?' she frowned at him. 'What's a nymph?'

'Never mind,' he replied. 'You better get back into town. I don't want you getting into trouble on my account.'

'It seems I'm always in trouble . . . either on your account or when you happen to be around. Why is that?'

'Maybe you're the high-spirited sort of girl who attracts trouble.'

She frowned. 'I certainly am not.'

'You could be a little headstrong too.'

'I'm as mellow as a butterfly!' she argued. 'It's the

100

people around me who are always making a fuss. So long as everyone does what I want and agrees with what I say, I get along with them just fine.'

He laughed at her assertion. 'Sparks, you are as rare as a blue moon and twice as precious.'

Jenny's ire vanished and she lowered her head demurely.

'You keep saying things to me that are . . . well, the kind of things that go with romance and courting.'

He stared directly into her twinkling hazel eyes.

'I expect to come courting, once your mother decides I'm no worse than a scalp-seeking savage.'

She met his gaze without flinching.

'You might have a long wait.'

'For a chance to hold your hand and call you my girl, I'd wait a lifetime, Sparks.'

Jenny straightened at his sincere tone of voice, then stood up so quickly, she dropped the glass. She rushed to bend over and pick it up, just as Dave did the same thing. It caused them to bump heads.

'Ouch!' she said, rubbing the top of her head. 'You Yanks got heads about as hard as a cannon ball.'

'Sometimes it hurts to be a gentleman,' he countered, holding out the lemonade container.

'Good night, Mr Kenyon,' Jenny stated pointedly, taking the glass.

'Yeah, good-night, Sparks.'

Then the girl whirled about and walked briskly back toward town. Dave watched her fade into the darkness and smiled to himself. Jenny was a lot of woman. He wondered if he was man enough to win her heart.

With a sigh, he concentrated on the sounds of the night once more. He couldn't afford to be off in dreamland and allow Gervaso's men to ride right past him. The time for romance had to wait. The first order of business was to survive the upcoming attack.

Jenny saw her mother standing outside the barn, waiting, arms folded, with a scowl of disapproval on her face. There was no way to escape the confrontation, so she continued her pace, summoning her courage as she drew closer.

'What's the idea of wandering off like that!' her mother demanded to know. 'I was worried you might have been kidnapped!'

Jenny stopped in front of her. 'I only took some cookies and lemonade out to the night guard. It's the least we can do, seeing's how we women are not allowed to keep watch by ourselves.'

'A man or boy only has to worry about being killed, Jenny. You have a whole lot more worries with men like those riding with Gervaso.'

'Yes, ma'am.'

Her mother was not finished. 'Besides which, I happen to know the guard out there is that miserable Yank.'

'He's our ally in this fight.'

'He's looking to shame you in front of the whole town,' she raved. 'And you ain't helping one bit – sneaking around to be with him behind my back!'

Jenny took a deep breath and boldly met her mother's wrath.

'I would have asked permission, Mother, but I'm

sure you would not have given it.'

'No, I wouldn't!'

'So, it's OK if he dies fighting to save our town and our lives, but not OK for him to share the fresh-baked cookies you made for everyone else?' Jenny gave a short negative shake of her head. 'Is it the Yankees who are spiteful and unfair-minded or us?'

'What about your friends, Jenny?' her mother countered. 'Do you want to sacrifice all of your friendships for one man?'

'I don't think anyone is going to consider the Kenyon boys as enemies, not after we share this fight together.'

'You're a headstrong girl, Jenny. I've hoped you would outgrow it as you got older.'

'You mean like the way you have over the years?' she challenged back.

'Did I mention, you're a brat too?'

'It's not my fault if I remind you of yourself when you were younger.'

'My mother died when I was fifteen.' Grace sighed. 'I wonder if I was enough like you to have contributed to her early demise?'

'It was only a couple of cookies, Mother.' Jenny softened her voice. 'It's not like we were out on a picnic or walking alone or anything.'

'Yes, but that's the next step, isn't it?'

'Once you allow I can start courting him,' Jenny replied, unable to withhold the hopeful note in her voice.

'Don't be holding your breath waiting for my consent,' her mother warned.

'I'm serious, Mother,' Jenny maintained. 'He told me he would ask for permission, once there was a chance you would say yes.'

'Maybe . . .' noting Jenny's immediate lift of spirits, she added, 'in about twenty more years.'

'Mother!'

'We have beds on the floor of the barn, along with some of the others from outside town. If we want to get any rest, we'll have to get to sleep before those who snore start sounding off.'

Jenny knew their discussion concerning the Yank was over. She gave a bob of her head.

'I'm ready when you are.'

'Come along then, Jen. Leave the glass on the table by the door and let's get to bed.'

They began to walk toward the barn.

'By the way, Mother, what exactly is a nymph?' Jenny asked.

Her mother showed her a frown. 'Where did you hear that word?'

'I was only wondering what it means?' She avoided an answer.

Her mother did not hide an immediate suspicion.

'It's most often used as a complimentary word, to describe a young, desirable and beautiful woman.'

Jenny's quiet response was a simple, 'Oh,' but her heart began to flutter and her pulse raced.

'Why do you ask, Jen?' her mother wanted to know. 'Who used the term?'

'It came up in a conversation,' she said, subtly trying to dismiss the subject. 'I was only curious as to whether it was good or bad.'

'I can guess about whom the name was intended.' Her mother continued her probe. 'It was you, wasn't it?'

Jenny was not a good liar, so she stuck with the truth.

'Yes.'

The news brought a groan from her mother.

'It was that Yank. He called you a nymph, trying to flatter you.'

'I don't know if he was trying to flatter me or not.'

'Well, I do, Jen,' the woman said. 'You put that guy out of your head. We have to get some sleep and then maybe fight a war. If we are all still alive when this is over, then we'll discuss whether or not you can ever associate with the Yank.'

'Whatever you say, Mother,' Jenny said, thinking she had made progress this day. Her mother steadfastly stood her ground concerning David, but she was weakening. The possibility of allowing him to court her had come down from *over my dead body* to a *maybe in about twenty years* and now: *if we are still alive when this is over*. Those were all steps in the right direction!

CHAPTER EIGHT

Rising from warm blankets and starting their ride before daylight had been a pain, but now Fryer looked over at Pudge and put on a wide, confident grin.

'This could be the start of you and me having our own command. We do this right and maybe Gervaso will send us out on our own every time.'

'That's right. Juan used to take men on his own all the time. With him gone, Angel needs another leader or two.'

'This is our chance.'

Pudge bobbed his head up and down.

'And we get first pickings of whatever we find.' He winked back at Fryer. 'Who knows? We might come across a stash of gold or a payroll of some kind.'

'Not to mention we get first pick of any good-looking woman who is willing to do anything to save her precious belongings.'

Pudge guffawed. 'Yeah, but we can't cross too many lines. We don't want the army making some kind of deal with Juárez. We wouldn't stand a chance against both the Mexican and the American armies.'

'We'll take it easy on the sorry souls of Three Forks, unless they put up a fight.'

'Right you are, *amigo*. We will pick their bones clean, maybe take a few hostages, then be gone within a few hours.'

Keen had been out in the lead, but he dropped back to ride alongside Pudge and Fryer.

'The main street of town is right around the next bend.'

'I remember this spot,' Fryer said. 'I recognize that big hanging-tree ahead.' He used his eyes to search the nearby woods and brush. 'I don't see any sign of life.'

'It's too early for most of those people to be up and around.'

'I'm still concerned about that yellow smoke we saw back in the hills,' Chico said from behind the three of them. 'It could have been a signal of some kind.'

'Yeah, right,' Pudge scoffed. 'The town hired some Indians to keep an eye on us. I'll bet we're about to run right into a Comanche war party.'

'Wood don't put off yellow smoke,' Chico argued. 'You should have let me ride up and see what it was.'

'Probably some rancher burning the body of a dead animal or something. No telling what he might have tossed on to their carcass to make it burn.'

'You worry too much, Chico,' Fryer chided him.

'Yeah, these people are mice for us wolves. They don't have the guts to take on Gervaso's men.'

Keen swung his head around as they crossed a

small ditch that ran across the road.

'Hey, why do you think someone dug—'

But their world turned unexpectedly violent!

Fire streaked across the path in front of them! Shouts to 'halt!' or 'don't move!' came from all around them. There was an immediate confusion among the five raiders.

Their horses sought direction or guidance and began to dance around and shy back from the fire. The men clawed for their weapons, as ropes and wire sprang up from the ground to form a barrier on either side. Behind them, a second wall of fire rose into the air. Even as they swung their guns about, searching for targets, a blinding barrage of fireworks exploded from both sides.

Streamers of brightly colored red, blue and gold shot past their heads. Explosions detonated under their horses and caused the animals to buck or rear up excitedly. Gervaso's men were engulfed in a shower of sparks, while bright balls of flame rose up from the earth. Then, when the fiery eruption dissipated, something fell from an overhanging limb. . . .

A hoard of angry wasps swarmed up from the broken nest, buzzing about in a fury, stinging both men and horses.

Chico was the first one thrown from his mount. He was dumped on his head, then screamed like a woman in labor as one of the animals stepped on his leg. Red forced his horse to jump the wall of flame to escape, but a rope settled about his shoulders and he was yanked off the animal's back and landed hard on the ground.

Fryer began to shoot wildly. He was in such a panic that he hit Keen right in his back pocket!

Keen howled in pain and Pudge cursed Fryer.

'Stop shooting, you blasted fool! You're going to kill one of us!'

Fryer ceased firing his gun and swatted wildly at the angry wasps. Meanwhile, Keen was also tossed from his spooked horse and spilled on to the ground. He tried to crawl away, but it was all he could do to escape the hoofs of the excited horses. He, Red and Chico were all crying out words of surrender.

'Drop your guns!' a voice shouted. 'Drop them and I'll throw smoke to get rid of the hornets!'

Pudge and Fryer were both quick to comply, tossing their guns on to the ground. They then used both hands to try and steady their frightened mounts.

Two grease-soaked rags were set afire and thrown into their midst. The wasps retreated or were too confounded by the smoke to continue their assault. Before the five men could get their bearings, they were surrounded by men with guns.

The fires, which had been burning across the road in front and back of Gervaso's band, died from lack of fuel and they were able to calm the horses. Within a few moments, the five men were disarmed and lined up in a single row. Chico had a broken leg and Keen was holding a hand over the wound he'd received to his behind. Red was on his feet, but he had not dared remove the rope around his shoulders.

'You three who can walk, lend a hand to the other

two,' Tom Delton ordered holding his gun on the men.

Dave waved the muzzle of his rifle.

'One wrong move by any one of you and we'll cut you all down.'

Fryer glowered at Dave when he spoke.

'You're the gun-slick from the hills. I recognize your voice.'

'Be thankful I was only aiming at your hat.'

Fryer gave a shake of his head.

'You people have just bought yourself a bushel of trouble. Gervaso is going to wipe you from the face of the earth.'

'Give your mouth a rest and lend a hand with your partners,' Tom ordered.

Fryer put an arm around Chico. With Pudge on the other side, they helped him hobble along on his one good leg. Red removed the rope so he could support Keen, who was able to limp along without too much discomfort.

'What are you going to do with us?' Pudge asked, after they had gone a short way.

'We're going to turn you over to the army,' Tom replied. 'They don't prosecute Yankees or their blue-belly supporters, but you sure don't fit into that category.'

'We was only riding through,' Pudge argued. 'We didn't do nothing.'

'I'm betting some of the people from Gloryville will recognize you boys. A couple of those people you beat and ran down with your horses died. That means you're all guilty of murder.'

Pudge bared his teeth in a sneer.

'When Gervaso hears you have us, he'll come with fifty men. There won't be enough left of your town to feed a handful of buzzards!'

'Stop it,' Dave said, 'you're scaring us to death.'

The men were herded into town and put into a storage house behind the saloon. It was sometimes used to store ice, so it had thick walls and no windows. With the door barred from the outside, it was as solid as any jail.

Chico had splints wrapped about his leg and Mrs Jardeen, who was a midwife and about the only one who did any doctoring around town, bandaged Keen's wound. The bullet had struck him at a sharp angle, so it had gone through his fleshy backside and missed the bone. The hardest part was trying to apply a bandage without making it look like the guy was wearing a diaper.

After a schedule was drawn up for guarding and tending the prisoners, Dave rode out to let his family know everything was all right. He would also tell his brothers they would have to keep watch until the army arrived. Their main concern presently, would the army arrive before Gervaso and his gang of cut-throats?

The freight and mail clerk gave a shake of his head.

'Sorry, boys, but the wire has been down for several weeks. We can't send a message from here.'

Kip was frantic. 'Didn't you hear what we said? Angel Gervaso is going to attack our town! We've got to have help!'

The man let out a woeful sigh.

'I'm really sorry, boys, but there ain't no way for me to send a wire. We don't have no pigeons or air balloons here for flying messages. Your best bet is the soldier boys over at Downy Junction. They'll have some way to get your message out.'

'How far is that?'

'Maybe sixty miles.'

Ricky looked at Kip. 'It will take us another full day and half the night to reach there. We're running out of time.'

'Yeah,' Kip agreed. 'Even if the town holds off the first assault, Gervaso will be there with his men before we can get help.'

'I wish there was something I could do, boys!' The clerk was sympathetic. 'With no railroad or stage station nearby, Downy Junction is about your only chance.'

'Is there some place we can exchange our horses?' Kip asked. 'We don't have any money, but we'll trade them back on our return.'

'I've got a couple out back,' the clerk offered. 'I'll have the missus put together a little chow for you boys too.'

'That would be great,' Kip replied. 'But we have to get on our way as soon as possible.'

'I'll show you where the horses are. While you change your gear, I'll grab you a little something to take with you.'

'We're mighty beholden to you, mister.'

'My sister's family were living over in Gloryville. They lost pertnear everything they owned in

112

Gervaso's raid. That bandit is everyone's problem. The sooner he is caught or killed, the safer everyone will be.'

Kip and Ricky followed the man out to a pole corral. He pointed out two good-looking mounts and left them to change over their saddles.

'I'm really concerned about the extra time this is going to take,' Kip told Ricky. 'The folks back at Three Forks will be thinking they only need hold out for a couple more days. With this delay, it's going to be more like four!'

'Nothing else we can do,' Ricky said. 'I took a look around when we rode in and have seen mostly women and children. I doubt there are more than a handful of fighting men in this whole town. We have to get the army to help.'

'Boy, oh, boy,' Kip worried aloud. 'I sure hope we're not too late.'

By the time Dave returned to town, the mood around town was festive and spirits were high. He had only time to eat something before his turn on guard duty. The warning was not spoken, but everyone knew there was added concern after taking Gervaso's men as prisoners. When the main body of the *comancheros* arrived, they would be expecting trouble. It would not be a handful of overconfident men, like the five they had locked away. The next time, the raiders would scout the town cautiously, expecting resistance. There would be no easy surprise a second time.

With the new threat, the guard was doubled. Dave

had hoped against good sense that he would be paired with Jenny, but it was not to be. There was resistance to using the girls for the forward sentry position. As a result, he ended up with Rex.

'What's your thoughts on when Gervaso will come?' Rex asked him, after a lengthy silence.

'If they are still camped near the mission, it's about a two-day ride,' Dave replied. 'Unless they have a spy around, who can report back at once, we ought to be safe enough for a couple days.'

'Yeah,' Rex agreed, 'they would have to give their boys time to return with their loot.'

'Be my guess.'

'You think Kip and the Mexican kid will get help back here before Gervaso's boys get here?' Rex asked, after another short silence.

Dave thought about it for a moment.

'I don't think we can count on it. Unless there is a troop close by, they will have to send a detachment of soldiers from the nearest post. It might be three or four days.'

'What'll we do if Gervaso arrives with fifty men?'

'Say a prayer and light a'shuck for the hills as fast as we can run.'

Rex chuckled. 'So much for the big hero.'

'Sometimes retreat is the only option, Rex. If the odds are too great, there's no sense in everyone in town being killed. We can always rebuild the town, but we can't bring any of the residents back to life, once they've been shot and killed.'

'I wanted to join up and fight in the war.' Rex changed the subject. 'I was old enough to go that last

114

year, but all of the fighting was so far back in the East – I didn't figure I'd get there in time to do any good.'

'From what my father has told me, the outcome of the war was pretty much decided by the time everyone took up sides,' Dave said. 'The South had the raw materials, but the North had all of the big factories and most of the real wealth. Given the Confederacy had only about one-third of the country's population, they were in a doomed position.'

'Yeah,' Rex agreed, 'I remember hearing some learned folks talking one time about how, if the North-west and California stayed out of the war, the Confederacy might have had a chance to win.'

Dave was sympathetic, but continued on the same logic.

'Once Missouri, Kentucky and Maryland sided with the North, the war was all over but the fighting.'

'Beating us on the battlefield don't make everything right, Kenyon,' Rex maintained. 'One bunch of states shouldn't be able to tell the others what they can or can't do.'

'Slavery is a tough issue to defend,' Dave replied. 'How many Texicans even had slaves?'

Rex shrugged his shoulders.

'I dunno, maybe one or two out of every few hundred. The only ones I ever seen were hire-outs, you know, a man with four or five slaves. They would take a job working the fields for wages, including the slave-owner. I guess there was some money to be made that way.'

'And the plantation owners?'

'I never even seen one close up,' Rex admitted.

'So, for the sake of a handful of slave-owners, your entire state went to war.' Dave uttered a negative grunt. 'It was the same in most Confederate states. The riches and power were controlled by the wealthy few, those who were making big money from slaves. The vast majority of the people who fought for the Confederacy didn't own slaves. They were fighting for their state's right to make their own laws. The result was a war which destroyed hundreds of towns and cities, laid waste to thousands of farms, plantations and homes, and caused the deaths of over half a million people.'

Rex obviously didn't like the conclusion.

'It is still a matter of principle, the right of every state to make their own choices.'

' "A house divided against itself cannot stand",' Dave argued. 'Those are the words of Abe Lincoln. How could our country remain free and independent among the world, if there were not a government to represent us as a whole?'

Rex uttered a sigh. 'I don't know all that much about politics.'

'The war was to emancipate the slaves of this nation, but it was also a struggle about money and power. You and me could have been like those men on the battlefields, killing each other because of our duty-bound honor for our own state. We would have been fighting a war for principle, while the few who owned slaves were concerned only about losing or sharing some of their profits.'

'I suppose you make some sense, Kenyon ... though I hate to admit it.'

'The truth doesn't take sides, Rex. It remains the truth, regardless of who speaks the words.'

Each sat in silence for a time, brooding with their own thoughts. Eventually Rex cast a sidelong glance at Dave.

'You know, Kenyon, as soon as we settled with Gervaso, I'm going to start courting Jenny proper.'

Dave gave him a half-grin.

'I was about to tell you the same thing.'

'Looks to be another war brewing between a Yank and a Johnny Reb.'

'Yeah,' Dave admitted, 'except this war will be settled by the fickle emotions of a pretty girl.'

Rex groaned. 'I think I'd prefer to step into a boxing-ring with you. I don't like the idea of letting Jenny decide for herself.'

'If it's any consolation, you've got her mother on your side.'

Rex laughed. 'I wish I could say the same for her brother. I've always pushed Kip around in the past. I'm afraid he'll back your play.'

'Makes us about even.'

'I'm better-looking than you,' Rex bragged. 'A little bigger too.'

Dave countered with: 'I'm more of a gentleman than you.'

'Jenny has to know it was you Kenyon boys who greased my wagon seat and ruined her dress.'

'She knows it was Cory's doing. I didn't know about or have anything to do with his dirty prank.'

Rex frowned. 'I was wondering why she didn't seem mad at you. I might have guessed you've been

117

slipping around behind my back.'

'You best stay on your toes, Rex. When it comes to Jenny, I'm not going to stand back and allow you a free hand to court her.'

'It looks as if the battle lines have been drawn, Kenyon.'

'How about we go with the old motto . . . may the best man win?'

'No thanks to that,' Rex responded. 'I want for her to pick me . . . whether I'm the best man or not!'

Angel Gervaso listened to Sauvage's bizarre report, his eyes growing wider with every word. When the Frenchman finished, he shook his head in wonder.

'Pudge, Fryer and the others were all taken without even firing a shot?'

'Well, Fryer *did* manage to shoot Keen.' Sauvage offered a dry retort. 'Right in the seat of his breeches!'

'A bunch of women and kids!' Gervaso exclaimed. 'They captured five of my best men, using fireworks, ropes and a nest of wasps!'

'I counted maybe four or five full-grown men. The others were kids.'

'A bunch of runny-nosed kids!' Gervaso about exploded. 'My fearless, terrible *comancheros*! taken prisoner by children!'

Sauvage put on a hard scowl.

'We can't underestimate them a second time, my leader.'

Gervaso rubbed his hands together, forcing himself to be rational.

'The men are split into three groups at the moment. We have only ten of us in camp. Can we handle those kids with such a small number?'

'They will need to guard the men they captured. As I told you, there were only a few real fighting men in their bunch.'

'They will send word to the army about the prisoners.'

Sauvage gave a careless lift of his shoulders.

'That is probable.'

'If they had wanted to kill them, they could have done that right off, instead of taking them alive.'

'I agree, my leader. And it will take some time to contact the American army. There is no telegraph at Three Forks – nor anywhere close.'

'We need to act quickly,' Gervaso said, 'to prevent our men from ending up in a Texas prison.'

Sauvage bobbed his head in agreement.

'It should take several days before any troops can arrive.'

'We need only enough time for us to pull our men out of there and squash the town like a bug under our feet!' Gervaso said with a snarl.

'I'll gather the men,' Sauvage said, hurrying off to rouse the camp.

Gervaso slammed an open fist into his palm.

'I'll show these Texicans what happens when they mess with Angel Gervaso and his men,' he vowed aloud. 'They will beg for mercy . . . before we burn the town down around their ears and trample them under the hoofs of our horses!'

CHAPTER NINE

'This is the idea,' Gramps said, showing the round piece of stovepipe to everyone. 'What does this look like?'

'A chimney for a pot-bellied stove,' Rex suggested.

Gramps frowned. 'I mean, what if you didn't know what it was?' he asked a second time.

Dave was next to speak up. 'I suppose, if you were to place it between a couple wagon wheels, it might look like a cannon . . . leastways, from a distance.'

The old man laughed gleefully. 'That's it exactly!'

'You're saying we should try and bluff Angel Gervaso this go around?' Rex asked.

'A couple of these, sitting in the middle of a barricade at the edge of town – he'll think we have enough artillery to blast him to kingdom come.'

'What if he don't?' Rex asked. 'What if he comes riding down the road with fifty men? We can't take on his whole army.'

'You remember what Ricky told us?' Dave spoke up. 'He said Gervaso's men were going to hit several small towns and villages. If that's the case, he might have his men spread out all over the country.'

'Meaning?' Rex wanted to know.

'Meaning he might only have a few men available. He can't wait for his gang to return from several different raids. If he does, the army ought to be here. His only chance to get his men back is to come straight away. He might only have a dozen or so men with him.'

'Even a dozen hardened, fighting men is a fair number,' Tom pointed out. 'We'd have a real chore trying to match their fire power.'

'That there's the exact reason we have to bluff them,' Gramps replied. 'With a couple of fake cannons and putting a few dummies in place and we can make it look as if he is facing thirty guns or more.'

'It would be risky,' Tom said. 'If the bluff didn't work, we'd be up to our necks in flying lead.'

'We can't expect to stop them with a handful of fireworks and a nest of wasps a second time,' Rex said. 'I say we open fire and take out as many of them as possible, including Angel Gervaso, if he's in the mix.'

'I don't know about you, Rex,' Dave said, 'but I don't have a clue as to what Gervaso looks like.'

'We'll hope it don't come to a shooting war,' Gramps said. 'I'm hoping we can cause them to retreat and wait for the rest of their gang. It will give the soldier boys more time to get here.'

Tom looked around and saw that most of the others appeared to be in agreement. 'You were ramrod for the first round, Gramps, and we did OK.

We'll follow your lead for another go.'

'Let's get to work,' Gramps told the group. 'I need a couple of men to help me with our cannons. The rest of you will work on stringing a tall fence between the buildings and setting up a barricade at the south end of the town. We also need a couple of the young-sters to keep watch for the smoke from the Kenyon boys.' He looked around and saw everyone was wait-ing for him to give the word. 'OK, let's get busy.'

Jenny moved over between Rex and Dave. Both of them paused to look at her.

'I don't see any black eyes or swollen faces,' she said, glancing from one to the other. 'Does that mean you two have made friends?'

'A truce might be a better term,' Dave replied.

Rex grinned. 'Yeah, we've done called a truce . . . at least, until this fighting is over.'

'I'm glad to hear it,' she said, obviously relieved. 'Gervaso and his men ought to be enough trouble for all of us.'

'What's your assignment?' Dave asked Jenny.

'I'm going to be one of the artillery men.' She laughed. 'Think I'll pass for a cannoneer?'

'Never met a cannoneer myself,' Dave said. 'Do they usually wear petticoats and have ribbons in their hair?'

'I'll look as big and ugly as you two, once I don a man's duds and big floppy hat.'

'What do you think, Rex?' Dave asked. 'Can she pass for a man?'

'I'm still trying to figure out how she can call the two best-looking guys in the valley big and ugly!'

'Yeah, there goes the notion she is perfect,' Dave replied. 'I'm afraid she needs a pair of spectacles so she can see.'

Jenny frowned appropriately. 'All I need is a mirror – so you two can see your own reflections!'

They might have enjoyed taunting one another for a short while longer, except that Tom approached the three of them. He was all business.

'You boys are with me. We're going to build a blockade to keep out Gervaso's boys. Keep your guns handy. We might not have any warning about them coming this time.'

'I'll get my rifle,' Dave said. 'It's over at the livery.'

'I'd better pick up mine too,' Rex also chimed in. 'I'll be back in a couple minutes.'

'Meet me in front of the general store and we'll get started,' Tom told them both. 'I'll round up some of the others to help.'

'Don't blow yourself up with that dangerous cannon,' Rex told Jenny.

Dave held back until both Tom and Rex had started to walk away. Then he winked at the girl.

'Be seeing you . . . Cannoneer Sparks!'

Instead of a scowl, Jenny actually smiled.

'Don't get yourself killed, Dave Kenyon. Rex needs a little competition to keep from thinking he's the only bull in the herd.'

Then they were both turning away to proceed to their respective jobs. There was a fight coming. If they were to have any chance at all, they had to be ready.

Sauvage pointed off into the distance.

'There's some yellow smoke,' he told Gervaso. 'I saw it before, when Fryer and Pudge led the men toward Three Forks.'

'A warning signal?'

'That would be my guess.'

'It means the farmers and ranchers are working together with the town.'

'Fryer said they checked most of the nearby farms and ranches. They didn't see a grown man among them.'

'Maybe they missed a few.'

'The town of Three Forks lost most of her men during the war.' Sauvage was thinking aloud. 'I would guess there is no more than a half-dozen men and a few boys.'

'What about riding into town from another direction?'

'It sits in a hollow, sided by steep hills to either side. We would have to ride twenty miles to get around either side to approach from the opposite end. We can do it, but it will take the better part of a day and it's hard country.'

'Then we will take them head on, but with caution. I'll send two men to scout ahead and we will keep a close eye out for any ambush.'

'Good idea.'

'Valdez! Toby!' He picked two of his men. 'Take the point!'

The two men obeyed at once, kicking their horses into a trot and pulling out in front of the small band.

'We will teach these mice not to play with cats!' he

124

declared. 'Once we free our men, we will take every-thing of value and burn the town to ashes. If we kill a few of their number, it will serve notice to the next Texas town not to stand against Angel Gervaso and his *comancheros*!'

They stood fifty meters to the front of the barricade, six men, including Rex and Dave. They were spread a few feet apart; each had a rifle in his hands, cocked and ready. When the first two raiders appeared, the sight of an armed force stopped them in their tracks. It took a few seconds before the rest of the number arrived.

Dave had one hand near the trigger guard of his rifle, the other up the forestock, ready to raise, aim and fire instantly. Tom held a double-barrel shotgun, while the others each had a carbine or rifle. Spread out in a line, the idea was to appear formidable.

'That's far enough!' Tom was the one who called the warning to Gervaso's men. 'Unless you want to be blown to pieces!'

A man astride a big black mare, clad in Mexican attire and a white sombreo, held up a hand to stop his small army. He then rode out a few meters in front of the rest of his band and glared at Tom, Dave and the others.

'I am Angel Gervaso!' he declared. 'You will release my men! Let them join us and I might decide to let you live!'

'Take a look over my shoulder,' Tom replied. 'Those cannon are filled with black powder and mixed shot of nails, pieces of twisted iron and small steel balls. One round from either of those guns will cut a swath through your men fifteen feet wide. You will look like so much ground meat!'

The leader gaped at the wagons and stacked boxes which blocked the street. His eyes became fixed upon the two cannons placed in this man-made barrier, both pointed in his direction. There were also a dozen or more men with rifles. He couldn't make them out clearly from the distance, but they were standing by, ready to open fire.

'I only wish the return of my men.' Gervaso tried again. 'Let them come to us and we will leave you in peace.'

'They are going to stand trial for what you did in Gloryville,' Tom replied.

'You are being very foolish!' Gervaso said, glowering at them again. 'I will destroy you! I will wipe you from the face of the earth!'

Tom remained poised.

'You have three choices. Drop your guns and surrender, turn tail and run or die right here and now.'

Gervaso's face reddened with his fury, but he swallowed his rage. He didn't have enough men to tackle a fortress and upwards of twenty armed men.

'We will be back,' he threatened. 'No one stands against Angel Gervaso's *comancheros* and lives to brag about it.'

Tom scoffed at his threat. 'You come back and it will be the end of both you and your *comancheros*!'

Gervaso raised his hand and waved for his men to follow him. Then he turned around on the trail and started back the way they'd come.

Dave realized he had been holding his breath. One wrong word, one twitch and it could have been a raging gun-battle. He quietly let the air out of his lungs, as the horses of the riders kicked up dust and disappeared along the road.

'Whew!' Tom exhaled loudly himself. 'I was afraid my heart was going to pound right through my chest.'

'You did a good job,' Dave told him. 'For a minute there, you had me believing we could have taken them in a fight.'

'It was good thinking, stopping them this far from town,' Rex put in. 'If they had gotten closer they would have seen the cannon were only pieces of black pipe and our army was made up of women and kids dressed like men.'

'It worked to drive them off, but I'm betting Gervaso will be back with his entire gang. Those soldiers better be here by then.'

'What now?' Rex asked.

'Dave,' Tom turned to him, 'you had best ride out and tell your brothers to keep watch from a different place. If Gervaso realized the smoke was a signal. . . .'

'I hear what you're saying,' Dave replied. 'When the bandit gang returns, they might try and prevent anyone from sending up a warning signal.'

'Got any ideas?'

'I'll look around and find another place where they can watch the trail without being at risk. I'll also make sure they don't stick around once they light the fire.'

'Sounds good.'

Dave left the others to pick up his horse. As he passed through the barricade he spied Jenny. She was wearing a pair of men's baggy trousers, a much-too-large cotton shirt and a hat that looked like it should have had holes for a mule's ears.

'That's a pretty good clown outfit, Sparks.' He stopped to tease her.

'I'm supposed to look like one of the cannoneers,' she replied huffily. 'Can't expect me to wear the dress you bought me while I'm manning a cannon.'

'The ploy worked,' he told her. 'Gervaso's eyes grew to the size of silver dollars when he got a look at our firepower.'

'I was a little worried about you men being out there . . . exposed like you were. If they had started shooting, you might have all been killed.'

'It was necessary to keep them far enough away so that they weren't able to recognize you ladies or the kids.' He tipped his head toward one of the makeshift cannon. 'And it wouldn't take a real close examination to deduce that our two stovepipes are not real cannons.'

'Even so, I was concerned for a few seconds there.'

Dave smiled. 'I feel right privileged, knowing you were fretting over my safety.'

A slight frown contorted her features.

'I didn't say I was fretting. And you weren't by yourself.'

'Oh.'

'After all.' She defended her position. 'If you men had gotten yourselves killed, then it would have been up to us women and kids to defend the town alone. I was merely pointing out how we were stronger with you than without you.'

'I see.'

She frowned. 'Don't you be making fun of me, David Kenyon!'

He chuckled at the immediate rise of her temper.

'Yep, Sparks was a good choice for a nickname for you.'

'Try and be nice and this is my thanks!' she fumed. 'I should know better than to associate with a Yank!'

'When this is over, I'd admire to come courting.'

Jenny maintained her fiery disposition.

'You've got about as much chance of that as Angel Gervaso himself!'

'Really?' He put on a serious mien. 'You won't even consider it?'

'No!'

'I'm serious, Sparks.'

'So am I!' she replied stubbornly.

Dave uttered a sigh of disappointment.

'If that's the truth, then I suppose there's no reason for me to hang around. I might as well get my horse and ride out.'

Jenny frowned. 'You wouldn't do that.'

He gave her a serious look.

'You're the only reason I'm here, Sparks. If there's no hope of my ever courting you, I reckon I'll head on back to the ranch.'

'You said this was your fight too!'

'That was for your benefit,' he said. 'I figured if I stood with you and the others, you might forget I was a Yankee. If I'm wasting my time chasing after you, then I'm not going to stay here and risk my neck for nothing.'

'Nothing!' She was aghast. 'You call the town of Three Forks nothing!'

'You're the only thing around here I consider to be worth dying for, Sparks. If I haven't got a chance with you, there's no need of my getting killed for a bunch of people who hate me.'

Jenny appeared flustered, unable to find the words to fire back, so Dave walked past her, to the livery. He got his horse from the corral and threw on a saddle. He had finished tightening the cinch, when he heard footsteps behind him. He paused to glance over his shoulder at Jenny.

'You don't mean it?' Her voice and expression were both uncertain. 'You're not really leaving?'

'Afraid so,' he said. 'Like I said, you're the only reason I'm here.'

'But . . .' He could see Jenny was squirming with her own conscience. 'What about the dance I owe you?'

He lifted his shoulders in a shrug.

'I won't hold you to it. There probably won't be a barn by Saturday anyway.'

'We had a deal,' she reminded him curtly. 'It was to be payment for the salt and sugar.'

Dave turned to face her squarely.

'I'll let you out of the bargain.'

Jenny lowered her eyes to the ground.

'Maybe . . . maybe I don't wish to be . . . let out of the bargain.'

130

'You just finished telling me that you wouldn't allow me to come courting.'

She raised her gaze to stare at him.

'Since when did you start listening to anything I said? I've been trying to drive you away since you Yanks arrived in the valley. It hasn't stopped you from chasing after me and saying all kinds of flattering things.'

Dave moved over to stand next to Jenny.

'I can only think of one way I might be persuaded to change my mind and stick around.'

Alarm sprang into Jenny's features. She was immediately suspicious.

'And what's that?'

'For a kiss from those perfect lips of yours,' he offered. 'One kiss and I'll stick here and die with the rest of you.'

Jenny took a backward step.

'No! I won't do it!'

'That's not much of a price to pay for a man's life.'

At her hesitation, he took the reins of his horse and raised his left foot to put into the stirrup.

'Wait!' she stopped him. 'I . . .' She visibly agonized with her good judgement, then blurted out: 'All right!'

Dave hid his smile of triumph, turned around and stepped over in front of her. He noted Jenny physically trembling, as he used one hand to remove the silly hat from her head.

'Pardon me, if I don't want to feel like I'm kissing a scarecrow,' he explained.

'Get it over with!' Jenny said, her teeth tightly

clenched, standing erect, her shoulders squared.

'You have to kiss back.' He made one more demand.

'Yes! Yes, I understand!' She appeared more anxious with each passing second. 'I know how to kiss!'

Dave lowered his head and leaned toward her. Jenny's chest lifted with her inhaling of a deep breath. She demurely moistened and pursed her lips into a slight pucker, tipped her head back slightly and closed her eyes. Dave's own mouth moved to a mere two inches away, ready to taste a small bit of heaven. . . .

'Say, Dave!' Rex's voice shattered the moment.

Jenny's eyes popped open. She backed up so quickly that she nearly lost her balance. Dave's own head snapped up and he wheeled around as Rex entered the barn.

'Tom says to stop by the store and pick up any supplies you might need for your brothers or family.' Then Rex paused, curious as to what was going on. 'Jenny?' he asked. 'What are you doing in here?'

She ignored his question and took a step toward him.

'What did you say?' she enquired. 'What about supplies for Dave's family?'

Rex still had an inquisitive look, but gave her an off-hand answer.

'Tom thought Dave's brothers and Ma might run low on rations while the boys are busy keeping watch and he's here with us guarding the town.'

Jenny swung around, boring into Dave with a smoldering glare.

'While he's *guarding the town*!' she grated every word.

Dave lifted his hands in a helpless gesture.

'Uh, I'm sorry, Sparks . . .' he began to confess, 'I thought you might. . . !'

Jenny's hand flashed before his eyes and Dave's left cheek was stung by a resounding slap. Before he could recover, she shoved the hat back on her head and stormed past Rex, on her way out of the barn.

'What the Sam Hill was that all about?' Rex asked, as soon as she was gone.

Dave rubbed his smarting cheek.

'That, my friend, was a reminder not to test Jenny's temper.'

Rex obviously didn't understand.

'Tell Tom thanks.' Dave returned to the business at hand. 'But we should have enough to get us by for a few more days.'

'Sure,' Rex said, still puzzled by Jenny's conduct. 'I'll see you when you get back.'

Dave lifted a hand in farewell and guided his horse out of the barn. He swept his gaze over the people on the street but did not see Jenny. When he reached the barricade, Tom was there.

'Keep a sharp eye, Kenyon,' he warned. 'Those bandits might have left a couple of men behind. They would like nothing more than to grab one of our number. They could either try and get information or use you as a hostage to trade for their men.'

Dave gave a nod of understanding.

'I'll stay off of the main road and use the back trail.'

'Good luck.'

Once a hundred yards down the trail, Dave turned his mount into the trees and began to thread his way to the crest of the hill that overlooked Three Forks. From there, he angled along the hogback ridge and was able to reach his house without exposing himself to anyone who might have been watching.

Even as he rode into the yard, he was still thinking about Jenny.

'So close . . . yet so far away,' he muttered to himself, thinking of the near kiss. 'Durned if that isn't the story of my life!'

CHAPTER TEN

'It isn't possible,' Sauvage told El Gervaso, having moved up alongside him. 'They could not have so many men.'

'Do my eyes deceive me?' Gervaso snarled a retort. 'Were we not staring down the muzzles of the guns from twenty men and two cannons?'

'It has to be a trick.'

'The trick would have been if they had started shooting, how would we have gotten out of there alive!'

Sauvage fell silent, but continued to frown in wonder.

'So many men, so many rifles . . . and the cannons! Where did they get two pieces of heavy artillery?'

'Maybe they were left behind when the army came through. Perhaps they are from a mission or fort used during the war with Mexico. Who can say?'

'What is the plan, my leader?' Sauvage asked.

'You slip back to keep an eye on these people and bring me a report. I want an accurate count of their number and strength. I will gather all of our men and we will meet at the main camp in three days.'

Sauvage gave a tip of his head to show he understood. As they reached a bend in the road and were well away from town, he neck-reined his horse into the brush and was lost from sight.

Gervaso was still seething. His blood boiled with the desire to crush the haughty Texicans under his heel. They had defied him, stood against him and his men, as if they were a superior breed. He would teach them a lesson none would soon forget. He would crush them like insects and leave the town in ashes. When he returned with his army, there would be no quarter for the people of Three Forks. No one would live to tell the tale of how Angel Gervaso had been forced to back down, to show his backside in retreat!

'They will pay for their defiance with their lives!' he vowed aloud.

Kip and Ricky had ridden without rest, changing horses where they could find a sympathetic rancher. Thirty miles from El Paso, they spied a column of troops on the road ahead.

'It's about time we got us a break!' Kip said, kicking his tired mount into a lope.

'Will they help us?' Ricky wanted to know, running his horse alongside. 'We sure haven't had much luck to this point.'

The officer at the head of the squad raised his hand to halt his small force. He appeared anxious, as the two boys rode up to them.

'Sir!' Kip began at once. 'We need help. There's

going to be an attack on Three Forks.'

'Is that you, Kip?' the officer asked.

Kip was startled. He looked hard at the soldier in charge.

'Captain Kenyon?'

'What's this about an attack?'

Kip and Ricky explained what they knew and how they had been sent to bring back help.

The captain listened and asked a question here and there. When he had all of the details, he summoned a corporal and gave him a message to carry back to headquarters.

'I was on my way to relieve a patrol,' the captain told the two boys. 'We'll pick up fresh mounts for you fellows and get under way.'

'But Gervaso has close to fifty men!' Ricky was the one to speak. 'We're going to need more than the few men you have here.'

'Not to worry, my young friend,' Captain Kenyon said. 'If the town can hold out until we get there, we'll have enough fire power to defeat Gervaso.'

'I hope there's still a town left.' Kip was somber. 'They didn't have many guns to take on a bandit army.'

'Let's get moving,' the captain ordered. 'Every minute we waste is another minute during which they have to fight off Gervaso's men.'

By the time the sun sank low on the horizon, Sauvage had picketed his horse in a cove and slipped in close enough to see the main street of town. He could make out the people clearly and soon began to smell the aroma from cooking as the people of Three Forks served up evening meals. From his hiding-place, he ate some jerky and drank from his canteen, all the while watching the movement on the street.

By the time darkness had covered the land, he had accounted for each grown man. He watched the change of guard and was puzzled. He counted less than a half-dozen men and two of them appeared to be crippled to some extent. What of those who had stood against Gervaso's approach? Where were the twenty-five fighting men they had faced?

Satisfied he knew the placement of the sentries, Sauvage began to make his way around the perimeter of town. Hidden by the darkness, careful in his movements, he worked to a point about even with the back door of the saloon. From his new position, he could see the barricade at the end of the street. There was light from a couple lanterns and a bit more from the windows of nearby buildings. It was enough for him to see that the cannons were not cannons at all, but pieces of rolled tin, set between two wagon wheels!

Sauvage cursed under his breath. He should have known! There was no artillery, no twenty men with guns! The townsfolk must have dressed up the young people and women to look like fighting men. They had invented two fake cannons and put up a false show of strength. There was only a mere handful of men in Three Forks!

Suffering an inner humiliation at being tricked, he spotted a lone man standing guard at the front of a storage shed. He recognized him as one of the six who had confronted him and Gervaso with rifles.

'So what are you guarding?' he whispered in his French tongue. 'Are you afraid someone will steal some ice? Or is that building serving as the town jail?'

Sauvage smiled, an idea forming in his head. Soon everyone would be asleep, except for the night guards. With so few fighting men to keep watch, they would be tired and less than alert. If he could manage a bit of luck, he would free Pudge, Fryer and the others. They would steal some guns and take over the entire town. What a prize for Gervaso! He could ride in like a king and set the first fire himself. To vindicate the humiliation done to them, they would burn Three Forks to the ground and kill anyone who stood against them.

It was a good plan.

It took longer than Dave had anticipated to find another place from where his brothers could safely send up a warning signal. Once they had decided on the how and where, he left them to return to town. It was so late that he probably should have stopped by his house and gotten a little sleep. However, he was scheduled for guard duty in town at midnight. He didn't want one of the others to have to take his watch. He knew he was no more weary than any of the other men.

Tom was at the first outpost. He stepped out from cover as Dave reached the old log next to the main trail.

'Glad to see it's you,' Tom greeted him. 'There's a full moon, but it doesn't put off much light. I've been able to hear you coming for the last five minutes.'

'Quiet night,' Dave replied. 'I didn't see or hear anything on the trail.'

'Your brothers all set?'

'The smoke will be more to the south-west than before, but they are camped at a knoll with no easy approach. They've got a good view of the main trail and can watch for anyone who might try to prevent them from sending up a warning.'

'Sounds good . . . unless they hit us at night.'

'Yeah, that means whoever is standing guard out here has to get off a warning shot or two.'

Tom looked at his timepiece.

'You're a little later than we expected. Rex will be wondering what's keeping you.'

'I'll get over there, soon as I put up my horse.'

'Thanks, Dave,' Tom said. Then, with a more serious tone, 'And I really mean that . . . thanks for all your help.'

'We're all on the same side, Tom,' Dave told him. 'We have been ever since our family moved out to the ranch.'

Tom gave a good-natured grunt.

'It means swallowing a little of our pride, but I guess we can learn to live with you Yanks as neighbors.'

Dave chuckled. 'Likewise about you Rebs, Tom.' Then he lifted a hand. 'Be seeing you.'

The barn was dark at the livery, so Dave stabled his horse in the main corral. He made sure there was grain, water and some hay, then headed over to the alleyway between the saloon and general store. Rex was probably wondering if anyone was ever going to show up to relieve him.

Suddenly, Dave heard the sound of voices, the noise of a scuffle or someone moving about. He hurried his step to the end of the passage and stopped. From the light filtering out of the saloon's rear window, he determined what was going on.

Rex was sprawled out on the ground, either unconscious or dead. A shadowy figure was in the process of opening the door to the storage shed. Even as he drew his gun, one of Gervaso's men started to come out of the makeshift prison.

'Hold it!' Dave shouted, taking aim at the first man.

But the man from inside had been given a gun – probably the one Rex had been carrying. He and the outside man both turned their weapons toward Dave.

There was a split-second decision to make. If Dave stood his ground, he might pin Gervaso's men down. If he ducked back for cover, the others would get out of the shed and infiltrate the town. Once they made it to the nearby buildings, they could grab hostages or find guns to arm themselves. Five or six hardened killers could feasibly take over the town.

Dave knew he had no real choice. With only the shadows of night for cover, he took aim at the two men. He fired just as the first man's gun roared back at him. Something slammed hard into Dave's left side. It felt like being hit full force with a double jackhammer. He staggered back a step from the severe blow, but still saw his target go down. The man fell against the shed door, knocking it shut, as he slid down to the ground. His body was there to pin the door closed, leaving Dave to deal only with the second man.

Dave aligned the sights of his gun again, as the other man fired several hasty shots at him. The flash gave off enough light for him to recognize the man called Pudge. Luckily, the man was shooting too fast to be accurate. One bullet kicked up dirt between Dave's feet, a second whistled past his head, while a third chipped wood from the saloon wall behind his right ear.

Dave locked the man in his sights and pulled the trigger again.

Pudge jerked back from the impact of the bullet, but he was not going down. He stretched his gun hand forward and continued to blast away.

There came an abrupt sting below Dave's right knee and the leg gave way. He sank to his knees, but managed to squeeze off his third round, making certain it was another good shot. Then the world grew dark and distorted before Dave's eyes. There was the acrid smell of smoke, mixed with the taste of dust. . . . He had the vague notion that he had fallen on to his face, but his brain was numb, unable to form a thought.

'What's going on?' he heard a distant voice shout.

'It's Dave!' came the reply. 'Looks as if he stopped a jail break!'

'Get some help! He's been hit. . . .' the voice trailed off, too faint for Dave to make out. Knowing Gervaso's remaining men were trapped inside the shed, he knew he had done his job. He ceased to battle against the black void which beckoned and was sucked into the vacuum of unconsciousness.

Jenny paced the floor, so worried that she was unable to sit still. Mrs Jardeen was not a doctor. She knew how to deliver a baby or patch a slight wound, as she had done for the injured *comanchero*, but remove a bullet? That was something she had never done.

Rex was sitting a few feet away. A bandage was wrapped about his head. He had been hit from behind with the butt of a gun. The clout had broken the skin and raised a fair-sized bump. He had been about half-conscious for the fight.

'It was my fault,' he said, looking up at Jenny. 'I let the guy sneak up on me. He took my gun without a fight.'

'Everyone is worn to a frazzle from keeping guard twenty-four hours a day.' Jenny exonerated his part in the attempted jail-break. 'None of us expected them to try and sneak someone in to free their men.'

'If Dave hadn't arrived when he did they might have taken over the town.'

'I'm sure Dave knew that too,' Jenny pointed out. 'He sacrificed himself to stop their escape.'

'I've badmouthed them Yanks ever since they arrived in Three Forks,' Rex said with an unveiled contempt. 'And now I owe one of them my life.' He heaved a sigh, 'Sometimes life is a real sack of spoiled spuds, you know?'

Jenny could not help but smile.

'I know exactly what you mean, Rex. Dave happened along to save my life too.'

'Sure hope he don't die.'

The smile vanished from Jenny's face. She again felt a terrible dread that burned inside her chest like a heated branding-iron. There were so many things she wanted to say to Dave. At their last meeting he had tried to prevail upon her to kiss him and she had slapped his face. It was not the last memory of Dave Kenyon that she wanted to keep in her heart. If he died before she could speak to him, she would forever hate . . .

The door to the bedroom opened abruptly and Mrs Jardeen came out.

'What's the verdict, Mom?' Rex asked, before Jenny could speak up. 'Is he going to make it?'

The woman did not hide her concern, but her voice was strong and moderately confident.

'The good news is, the bullet went right through his upper shoulder. There was no froth from a lung visible, so I believe it was a clean shot. The leg wound was not too severe, it hit mostly flesh and nicked the shin bone. If he hasn't lost too much blood and doesn't develop an infection, he should recover OK.'

Jenny went over to Mrs Jardeen and hugged her tightly.

'Thank you,' she murmured, trying not to sob the words. 'Thank you for tending to him.'

When she drew back from the woman, Mrs Jardeen displayed an encouraging smile.

'He's a tough young man. I don't think he's going to let a couple little scratches get the best of him.'

'Can I see him?'

'He isn't conscious, but you can sit with him if you like.'

Jenny started for the bedroom, but Mrs Jardeen stopped her.

'If he does wake up, there's a pitcher of water next to his bed. See that he drinks as much as he can.'

'Yes, yes, I will!' Jenny said quickly. Then she was hurrying through the door.

'So, Mom.' She heard Rex speak to his mother in a dry sort of voice. 'Who do you think Jenny is going to want to come courting, me or the Yank?'

She didn't wait for the answer, but closed the door and went over to the bed. The lamp had been set so low that she could barely make out Dave's face. It appeared drawn and ashen in color. However, his breathing was deep and even. She decided that was a good sign.

There was a chair in the room, so Jenny pulled it over to within a couple feet of the bed and sat down. She didn't care how long it took, she intended to be there when Dave Kenyon woke up.

Angel Gervaso stood at the edge of the campsite, just beyond the light of the fire. He was worried about Sauvage. The man should have returned by this time. He heard the steps of someone and glanced over his shoulder. It was Jubal Brown, one of his long-time men, who had come to speak with him.

'We have already lost a full day,' Jubal said. 'How long do we sit and wait?'

'If Sauvage is not here by morning, we will ride across the border.'

'Is this a wise course of action?' Jubal asked. 'Those townspeople have had plenty of time to summon help. We might be riding into a trap.'

'We shall take great care in our approach,' Gervaso assured him. 'Before we enter the valley of Three Forks, we will send scouts ahead on either side of the main road. I'm certain the town has a sentry in the hills, one who warned of our advance last time. We won't let that happen again.'

'And if the soldiers have come to their aid?'

'Rest assured, my friend, we will gauge our opposition, before we launch any attack. If there are too many soldiers or if too many fighting men have joined their ranks, we will leave Three Forks alone and find another target.'

'What about Fryer, Pudge and the others?'

'They were foolish enough to be caught. If we can't take the town, they will have to take the punishment or escape on their own.'

'I'm glad we're moving out in the morning,' Jubal said. 'The men grow anxious for action.'

'The town of Three Forks will give them the action they desire. If there are no soldiers, we will tread our horses over the bodies of those impudent Texicans. We'll take everything of value, including the women and children. If the Texas government will not pay a ransom to get them back, I know of a few places where we can sell the white slaves.'

'We could use a few more young ladies around here,' Jubal said, showing his white teeth in a smirk. 'Our own women grow weary of feeding and caring for so many men. They would welcome the help.'

'We will see,' Gervaso promised. 'Once we take the town, I will leave the choosing of slaves up to you.'

'I'll spread the word,' Jubal said. 'The men will be ready to ride at first light.'

Gervaso gave a nod of approval, then turned to stare back out into the night. It was still disturbing that Sauvage had not returned. The French man was his best scout. If the weasels of Three Forks had caught or killed him, it would be a great loss to his gang.

Thinking along such lines the worry was crushed, replaced by anger. That one tiny, ant-hill of a town had bested his men and made a fool of him personally. First, his cousin had been killed by an unknown man who hid in the bushes. Then, his advance group of men got taken prisoner without a fight, tricked and captured like schoolchildren. Then, on his own approach, he had underestimated the town's strength and taken too few men. He had been forced to show his tail and retreat, something he had never done before. And now, Sauvage, his key reconnoiterer was missing. The logical conclusion was that the Texicans had either killed him or he was now a prisoner too.

The score was four victories for Three Forks and zero for him and his men. It was not a record Gervaso could digest. Indeed, he felt a gnawing inside his stomach, a continuous torment that would not quit. He needed a major victory against the fighting men at Three Forks. He would crush them under his horse's hoofs and watch the town be reduced to ashes. Nothing would stand in his way this time. His triumph would restore his pride and free his captured men. There would be no witnesses to testify to his defeats.

CHAPTER ELEVEN

Dave felt something moist caress his brow. With a gentle touch, the damp coolness traced a path about his face and continued along the side of his neck.

'Don't you be fretting, David,' a winsome voice murmured. 'You're going to be just fine.'

Dave's eyelids felt encrusted with lead weights. He languidly became aware of his surroundings, listening with his ears and picking up an odd mix of aromas with his sense of smell. There was something astringent, like alcohol or medicine, but also a honey-sweet fragrance, like a perfumed soap or rose-water.

'Are you trying to wake up?' the voice asked.

Dave kept his expression blank and managed to maintain an even breathing. After a moment, he made out an audible sigh.

'Well, you're certainly not as tough and indestructible as I always thought.' Jenny was mildly critical. 'One little bullet and you end up bedridden for sixteen hours. I swear, if I didn't know better, I'd think you are avoiding . . .'

Dave mustered forth the strength to pry open his

eyes. Jenny was looking right at him and she immediately stopped in mid-sentence.

'Avoiding what?' he asked in a voice that was both
husky and dry.

'Nothing!' Jenny said a bit too quickly. 'Do you
want some water?'

'Please,' he replied.

Jenny poured some from a pitcher into a cup and
then held it to Dave's lips. He took small sips, but,
once the refreshing liquid had soothed his parched
throat, finished his question.

'What have I been avoiding, Jenny?'

'You shouldn't call me by my first name. It isn't
proper.'

'I reckon my intentions toward you are proper
enough.'

'David!'

'See?' He worked the corners of his mouth up into
a tight grin. 'You must agree, or you'd have called me
Mr Kenyon.'

'It was a slip of the tongue, nothing else.'

'Did we get them all?' He changed the topic.
'Gervaso's men, I mean.'

'You stopped their escape. Both of the men you
shot are dead.'

'Lucky shooting on my part,' he said. 'I'm not all
that good with a handgun.'

'Standing there and being a target for them was
not the brightest thing you could have done either.
Why didn't you call for help?'

'When I arrived, the door was already open to the
storage shack. I didn't want the others to get loose. I

figured I had to stop the man in the doorway, in order to keep the rest of them pinned inside.'

'Yes, well, it worked. Rex said the one bandit – Pudge, I believe it was – fell against the door and blocked it shut. Tom and some of the others arrived before any of the imprisoned men could push their way out.'

Dave closed his eyes again as a wave of pain washed over his left side. He tested his legs and could feel the tight bandage around one lower leg.

'Guess I didn't get hit too bad.'

'A couple inches lower and the bullet in your shoulder would have gone right through your cold, black heart.'

Dave blinked at the pang of agony and took a slow, deep breath. It seemed to relieve the pain. Jenny was close enough for him to reach out with his right hand and take hold of her wrist. A look of surprise rushed on to her face as he moved her hand to place her palm right over his heart.

'Feel that?' he said.

Jenny appeared flustered and embarrassed.

'Feel what?'

'My cold, black heart,' he said. 'Are you sure it's really cold?'

Jenny jerked back her hand. 'I-I . . .'

'My heart beats only for you, Sparks,' Dave told her softly. 'If you can truthfully say you don't have any feelings for me, I'll stop chasing after you.'

'And if I can't say exactly one way or the other?'

He smiled. 'We can settle that quick enough.'

'How?'

'You only have to kiss me.'

Jenny frowned. 'You tried to pull this kind of stunt when you rode out to confer with your brothers! I won't be tricked or blackmailed into kissing you!'

'Then how about because you owe me one?'

'Owe you one?' she cried. 'What do you mean, I owe you one!'

'Just what you were talking about, Sparks. It was over at the livery, when you were going to kiss me so I would stay and fight.'

'You had already promised Tom and others you would fight with us.'

'It makes no difference,' he argued. 'You were going to give me one kiss to keep me here. You never paid up.'

'It was a ruse!'

'And you slapped me for the ruse,' he reminded her. 'I got punished for the scheme, but I never got paid properly in the first place. You ought either to take back your slap or give me the kiss you owe me.'

Jenny laughed at his preposterous logic.

'Of all the low-down, double-dealing, sneaky, under-handed ideas! I'm supposed to owe you a kiss, because I learned of your trick before you got what you were after. That's the most lame argument I ever heard.'

Dave sighed. 'How can I ever tell our kids that their mother was not a woman of her word? What kind of lifelong scar do you think that will create for them?'

She was incredulous. 'What do you mean, *our kids*!'

'You gave your word and you broke it. Trick or not, you slapped me for something that never happened.'

151

'I slapped you for trying to deceive me into kissing you.'

'And if we had already kissed?' he challenged her. 'Would you have done anything more than give me a good swat?'

Jenny was confounded by his logic.

'I refuse to let you make me out to be in the wrong. You're turning the whole situation around and making it look like I didn't have the right to slap your face.'

'I grant you had the right to slap me.' He continued his debate. 'But only after you allowed me the kiss. No kiss, no slap – it's only fair.'

'Oh, for the love of . . .' Jenny ceased to battle. Quite without warning, she leaned over and planted a firm kiss on his lips. After a few seconds, she raised up and bore into him with a heated gaze.

'All right!' she declared. 'Now, are we even?'

Dave worked hard to get his brain to function.

'Yeah . . . I reckon so.'

Jenny stood up.

'Fine,' she grated the word. 'Then I'm going to get some sleep. I've given up enough of my time for one little bullet wound.'

'Two!' he reminded her.

'Good-night,' she said, and stormed from the room in a huff.

Dave stared at the door for a long time after she had left. In spite of the pain throbbing in his shoulder, he smiled.

The following morning the door burst open and

Cory and Adam hurried into the room. Dave had been lying in bed with his eyes closed, but he was not asleep. He turned his head and saw the two were flushed from excitement.

'Davy!' Cory exclaimed. 'You've been shot?'

'It isn't bad,' he told them. 'What are you doing here? Who is keeping watch?'

'No need to keep watch any more, big brother,' Cory replied. 'We've run out of time.'

'Gervaso?'

'They had men scouring the hills to either side of the main road. We didn't dare send a signal, so we came into town to warn everyone in person.'

'How many men?'

'Couldn't get a complete count, what with scouts working through the hills, but there must be thirty or more.'

'We don't have a chance.' Adam spoke up. 'There's no way we can defend this here town with so few men.'

Dave used his good hand to push himself up to a sitting position.

'Hand me my shirt,' he told Adam.

'You don't look in any condition to fight,' Cory said.

'I killed Gervaso's cousin, Juan. Next, we captured several of Gervaso's men, and finally, we turned him back with our trick cannons and phony riflemen. He is going to want a total revenge, a victory that will leave no one standing.'

Adam helped Dave on with his shirt and boots. By the time he was ready to stand, Dave was already sweating from the pain.

'You boys got your rifles?'

'We've got them,' Cory replied. 'But this is crazy.'

Dave took a deep breath and tested his injured leg. The bullet had nicked the bone, but he was able to limp along at a snail's pace.

'You can stay and help,' Dave told his brothers. 'If we can't hold them off once they have breached the barricade and are sure to take the town, you two light out for home.'

'What about you?'

'I'll be doing the same thing,' he lied, knowing he would die defending the lives of the people in Three Forks.

The three of them made their way out to the street. Tom and Gramps came over to meet them, both of them surprised to see Dave on his feet.

'They's comin' up the road, moving slow,' Gramps announced. 'Looks to be thirty or forty of them.'

'You able to hold a gun, Dave?' Tom asked. 'You look pretty pale.'

'I can fight,' Dave told him. 'My brothers are throwing in with us too. It'll give us a couple more guns.'

'We'll never be able to hold off so many men,' Tom told him. 'You should take your brothers and get out of town.'

'This is our town too,' Dave replied. 'We'll hold out as long as we can.'

'I guess we're as ready as we'll ever be,' Gramps said in a determined tone.

Tom explained their strategy.

'The women have taken positions on the roof of the store and saloon. They will have a good field of fire for covering us at the barricade and be hard to get at.'

'Rex is going to hold his position at the storage shed.' Gramps continued to outline their battle plan. 'He can watch one side of town and help cover our flank on that side. I've put Ben Stokes and a couple of the kids who can shoot on the opposite side.'

'Sounds like you've got our defense ready.' Dave commended their actions.

'With you three, we might turn back the first charge.' Tom lifted a shoulder in a shrug. 'I don't know about after that.'

Dave set his teeth against the throbbing ache that raked the left side of his chest. He tucked in his arm and placed his hand over the wound. It seemed to lessen the streaks of pain.

'Let's see what kind of grit this bandit army is made up of.'

They started to move forward, a handful of determined men. They knew there was no chance to win against Gervaso, but they would die defending their town and the people they loved.

'Hey!' Adam suddenly shouted. 'Look there!'

Dave looked at his youngest brother and saw he was staring down the street behind them. It hurt to look over his shoulder, so he took a step to turn. What he saw caused the pain to evaporate. It was Kip and Ricky . . . and his father – at the head of twenty or more troopers!

They rode up to within a few feet and stopped. Captain Kenyon smiled down at Tom.

'You don't mind if we take a hand in this little war of yours, do you?'

Tom laughed. 'Never figured I'd ever be so glad to see that blue Yankee uniform, Will. Another five minutes and you would have been too late!'

'Gervaso is that close?'

'They're almost at the bend in the road,' Tom told him. 'They'll be here any minute.'

'Sergeant!' William barked the order. 'Disperse the men, hide the mounts, and prepare for the engagement.'

'Yes, sir!' the sergeant replied.

'The livery is over this way.' Cory spoke up. 'The corral is behind the barn, so it will hide your horses.'

William climbed down and gave the reins of his horse to one of the troopers. He looked at Dave, concern shining brightly.

'Are you injured, son?'

'It's only a scratch or two, Dad,' Dave replied. 'I didn't seen any reason to baby the wounds.' He chuckled. 'Didn't figure to live long enough to ever heal.'

'We'll sneak our men forward and take up positions at the barricade. When Gervaso arrives, we'll have a rude surprise waiting for him.'

Tom, Gramps and the two boys hurried off to get into position. Will stayed with Dave, moving for cover at a much slower pace.

'We can handle this without you, Dave,' his father said. 'You don't have to be out here.'

'I'll do my share, Dad. I'm the one who helped start this.'

'Yes, Kip told me about you saving his sister from three of Gervaso's men.' He narrowed his gaze. 'Should I read something in to that?'

156

'Like what?'

'What do you mean "like what?" ' a familiar voice spoke up from behind them.

Jenny had approached them without being heard. William regarded her with a look of surprise, while Dave frowned.

'You're supposed to be with the women, up on the roof of the saloon.'

'I'm a better shot from closer up,' Jenny explained, moving over to stand next to Dave. 'Besides, someone has to reload for you, David. You're going to be slower than the change of seasons with a bad shoulder.'

Will smiled at her, then winked at his son.

'It would appear you've made peace with the ex-Confederate populace while I've been away.'

'You could say that, Dad. This here is the woman I'm going to marry.'

Jenny gasped in shock.

'I never said I would marry you!'

'What she means is, we haven't got around to setting an exact date or anything.'

'You've never even come courting!' Jenny was still fussing. 'How can you be saying something like that! My mother is going to have an apoplexy!'

'Let's get in position,' Will said, turning to the business at hand. 'I don't want them to see me or my men until it's too late.'

Dave began to limp.

'Maybe you should help steady me, Sparks. Hate to fall flat on my face and re-injure the wound in my chest.'

'Darn your arrogant hide!' Jenny snapped, as she put an arm around Dave. 'You're going to pay for this!'

They moved to a place behind a pile of grain sacks, which had been filled with sand. There was a portal for shooting and Dave could rest on his good knee to aim. After Jenny helped him into position she glowered at him.

'What's the idea of telling your father you are going to marry me?' she hissed the words in a hushed voice. 'We've never even talked about an engagement.'

Dave cocked his head and smiled at her.

'You didn't refuse,' he teased. 'I've got to read that as a positive sign.'

'You might have asked me proper.'

Dave grew serious, peering directly in to her eyes.

'I've been in love with you ever since we moved to Three Forks, Sparks. I might not have said the words out loud, but my heart has been yours since the first time I set eyes on you.'

She appeared flustered and surprised at his confession.

'Really?'

'As soon as this fight is over, I'll be asking your mother for permission to come courting.'

Jenny gave a negative shake of her head.

'My mother will never agree to let me be courted by a Yank.'

Dave didn't have time to argue his case. Gervaso's men appeared, guns in the air, charging at them at full gallop!

'Hold your fire!' William called out. 'Wait until they are in range.'

The bandit horde was nearly forty strong, all opening fire, shooting wildly at the barricade. They approached like a swarm of angry bees, ready to sting and slaughter all who stood in their path. . . .

'Now!' William shouted.

The volley of gunfire rocked the valley walls. The Union troops were not battle-hardened, but many of them were good shots. Gervaso's men spilled from their saddles, horses tumbled, and there were cries of agony and death.

Dave couldn't identify Gervaso in the mêlée, but he picked out a man on a white horse. His shot was true, knocking him from his mount with a single round.

The charge was stopped by the barrage of gunfire. In less than a heartbeat, a dozen or more men had been taken out of the fight. Most of the *comancheros* stopped and sent shots at the barricade, but several more saddles were emptied.

Gervaso's band of killers turned to retreat . . . only to run into a second army: Mexican Juaristas! Those who didn't surrender were downed in a hail of gunfire. The entire battle took less than two minutes, but it was enough to obliterate the *comanchero* gang.

'I had a wire sent to Benito Juárez and told him about Gervaso,' William explained to Dave. 'These men have raided both sides of the border for the past couple years. I got permission for him to cross the border and take prisoners.'

'Prisoners?' Dave asked.

'His men will arrest the Mexicans and return them for trial in Mexico. We will arrest the others and hold them for trial here in Texas.'

The troopers moved out, collecting the wounded, preparing the dead, and taking prisoners. After an hour or so, the Mexican contingent took several men into their custody and parted company.

Dave would have liked to watch, but Jenny insisted he return to bed.

'I'm all right,' he argued with her. 'The wound hardly hurts at all.'

'That's not what you said a few minutes ago,' she reminded him. 'As I recall, you needed to lean on me to get to your station at the barricade.'

He grinned. 'That was only so I could put my arm around you.'

Jenny put on the appropriate frown.

'Is this what I have to look forward to after we're married? You always trying to find some excuse to kiss me or put your arms around me?'

'I'm afraid so, dar'lin,' he admitted. 'I intend to kiss and hold you every chance I get.'

She laughed, her eyes bright with a mischievous glint.

'That's one promise I'm going to hold you to, David Kenyon . . . for the rest of my life.'

Lacking the proper words of endearment, Dave demonstrated how he felt about such an arrangement – he took Jenny in his arms and kissed her. The pain pounded in his injured leg, his shoulder was on fire, but the discomfort didn't bother him one little bit.